ONE NIGHT ONLY

M. S. PARKER

BELMONTE PUBLISHING, LLC

This book is a work of fiction. The names, characters, places and incidents are products of the writer's imagination or have been used fictitiously and are not to be construed as real. Any resemblance to persons, living or dead, actual events, locales or organizations is entirely coincidental.

Published by Belmonte Publishing LLC

ISBN-13:978-1981454990

ISBN-10:1981454993

ONE
SAVANNAH

It was too fucking hot outside, but it had been a hell of a week, and I needed to unwind. And not the eating ice cream and binging on *Game of Thrones* kind of unwinding. I needed dancing, drinking, and fucking, though I wasn't particular about the order.

The sun was almost down by the time I stepped back outside, but New York City was still sweltering. Then again, it was the end of June, so the heat wasn't surprising. Even in my barely-there dress, my skin glowed with a thin sheen of sweat when I climbed into the cab. I gave the driver the club's address and grimaced as the backs of my thighs stuck to the seat despite the air-conditioning.

I grew up in Indiana, so it wasn't like I wasn't used to the heat, but there was something different about a suburban summer in the Midwest as opposed to the Big

Apple. Like all the worst parts of sun and heat and humanity came together in the worst possible way. It was one of the few things I didn't like about the city. Everything had to have some downsides, right?

"Savannah!"

My best friend was shouting before the cab even pulled to a stop.

"Savannah Birch, you sexy little bitch, get your ass out of there and get over here!"

Oh shit, he was drunk already.

"Here." I handed the driver a couple bills. "Thanks."

I'd barely gotten two steps away before six feet, five inches of gorgeous gay man enfolded me in an entirely too sweaty hug.

"How much have you had to drink?" My voice was muffled as I tried to push him away. I loved him, but it was too fucking hot for this mess.

"You were late," Everett explained as he hooked his arm through mine and practically pulled me to the door. "So Lei and Lorde decided we needed to play a drinking game. I'm losing."

I shook my head. "You know, one would think that seven years with those two would've taught you a thing or two."

He gave me one of his devastating grins and winked at the bouncer as we went inside. He always got flirty and flamboyant when he drank, which was usually why Lei and Lorde liked to make it happen. A drunk Everett was a sight to behold.

Everett and I had been inseparable since the first day of kindergarten when Titus McPherson stole my Captain America lunchbox. I'd gone after him, but not before Titus spilled the contents everywhere and stomped all over them just because my brother, Jonathan, had called his brother a booger eater, which was, of course, a deadly insult for a manly preschooler to offer. I'd been ready to knock out a tooth or two when this scrawny little thing with platinum blond hair and the greenest eyes I'd ever seen came up, shoved Titus hard enough to knock him on his ass, then said I could share his lunch.

He officially came out to me in seventh grade, but I'd suspected his sexual preferences when he joined me in mooning over whichever boy band was the most popular at the time. Fortunately, I'd never harbored any romantic feelings for him, so I was able to be totally supportive after he had *the talk* with his parents.

"You're late." Lorde Mayfair and I bonded over a shared birthday when we met at NYU freshman orientation. She had a degree in Metropolitan studies, but currently worked as a sales clerk at a high-end fashion boutique while she decided what she wanted to do with the rest of her life. As a result, she never quite understood the dedication the rest of us had toward our careers.

"And you look amazing," I said as I took in the cute

sundress that did wonders for her pleasantly plump figure. With her youthfully cute face, short chestnut brown waves, and blue-green eyes, she still got carded even though she was twenty-five.

"So do you," she said as she gave me a loose hug before sitting back down.

"See, Everett, some people understand personal boundaries," I teased as he plopped down in the booth. He stretched his arms out across the top of the seat and ruffled Lorde's hair.

"Hey, I can't help it that you're so huggable," he countered. "Like a teddy bear. An angry teddy bear."

I glared at Lorde, who gave me a wide-eyed, innocent look, and pointed to the fourth member of our party.

Lei Oshiro was the most unassuming member of the group, and the youngest at twenty-four. A second-generation Japanese-American, she spoke the language fluently and often used it to confuse men who wouldn't quite take no for an answer. Because she was on the quiet side, most people didn't realize that a devious personality lurked behind those nut-brown eyes.

She shrugged. "You know how easily I get bored."

"Time to catch up!" Everett announced as he jumped up. "I'm buying this round."

As he headed toward the bar with our orders, I fanned my face. The air conditioning was on in here, but there were so many bodies packed into one place that it barely made a difference. I'd pulled all of my curls up into a sloppy sort of up-do that was both practical and appealing, so I supposed it could have been worse.

"Is Robert meeting us tonight?" I leaned close to Lorde so I could ask the question without yelling. The new song the DJ was spinning had the sort of pounding beat that made talking nearly impossible, but dancing a near inevitability.

Lorde shook her head. "Business trip to the West Coast. Won't be home until Sunday afternoon."

She genuinely looked sad, and I couldn't really blame her. She and her fiancé had been together for six years and would be tying the knot in December. His name was Robert Huntington III, and most people would expect that, with a name so dickishly presumptuous sounding, he'd be a total asswipe, but he was actually a really great guy. Lei and I always said that we were both single because Robert set the bar far too high when it came to boyfriends.

"I guess that means you'll be dancing with us all night." I picked up the glass that Everett had just set down in front of me. I downed it in a couple gulps, then grabbed Lorde's hands and pulled her onto the dance floor.

It was time to forget about the week and all the shit assignments I kept getting at work. I was here to have some fun.

As a tall, dark-haired hottie sidled past me, I gave him a lingering look. Yeah, I needed to get laid too. I hadn't had an actual relationship in nearly two years, but I had no problem with one night stands if I had an itch that needed to be scratched.

And I'd been itchy for nearly a month.

I could take care of things myself, but there was something to be said about having a hard body over you, underneath you, against you...I blew out a breath. Damn. I definitely needed to hook up with someone tonight, or I was going to spontaneously combust. One of the biggest benefits of living with Everett was that I didn't need to worry about the danger of bringing a stranger home. He was usually the most laid-back, easy-going person I knew, but he could be downright scary when it came to protecting his friends.

Judging by the way he and a lanky brunet were grinding against each other, I wouldn't be the only one getting lucky tonight. Good for him.

"I LIKE YOUR HAIR," I said as I clung to the arm of Lewis – Leonard? Leon?

I'd call him *L*, I decided. Made things easier to remember.

As he leaned down to take my key from my hand, I patted the man bun on the top of his head.

"It's poofy." I giggled, then cursed. "Fuck, fuck, fuck! I wasn't supposed to drink this much tonight."

L stopped with the door halfway open and gave me a concerned look. "Do I need to be worried?"

I shook my head. "Still completely capable of making an informed decision." I grinned at him and patted his hair again. "I just get a bit...*silly* when I've had a few."

His dark eyes twinkled as he laughed, but he didn't turn around and go home, so I figured we were good to go. And boy did I ever want to go. I was going to ride him like a pony.

He better be able to keep up or silly drunk was going to become pissed drunk.

As soon as I kicked the door closed, I was on him, tugging at the skin-tight t-shirt that showed every muscle in his lean torso. He was a bit pretty for my tastes, and I usually didn't go for the sort of guys who had man buns and beards, but I was a little bit tipsy and a lot horny, so this was going to happen, pretty boy or not.

He was talking as he stripped off the rest of his clothes, but I wasn't really paying that much attention. It was all "you're so hot" and that sort of thing. I didn't really care about the compliments, and I wasn't interested in getting to know him. I just wanted to fuck him until I could no longer think.

Suddenly, Everett's laughter echoed in the hallway,

followed by the lower, more sensual laugh of the guy he'd been hanging on all night.

"Dammit! Bedroom," I said as I grabbed L's wrist. "Gotta go quick."

His pants were around his ankles, hindering his ability to walk as I practically dragged him after me, and I could barely keep myself from laughing. I mentally cursed my friends, and vowed to get them back for letting me get loopy-drunk.

"We can do it out here," he said. "You got a nice couch."

"I also have a roommate." I looked over my shoulder and giggled at the hopeful expression on his face. "Who's a guy. Bringing home another guy."

"Bedroom," L agreed with a laugh.

He was still struggling with his pants when I pushed him back onto the bed.

"Time's up," I said as I reached up behind my neck and untied the strap holding my top. "I'm in charge."

His eyebrows went up as his gaze dropped to my bare breasts. "Babe, you can be in charge of me any day."

“I fixed him with a mock glare. "Shh. No talking. Just fucking."

He pretended to lock his mouth and throw away the key. Then he watched as I climbed onto the bed, my eyes on the prize. Silly or not, I knew what I wanted, and tonight, I was going to get it.

About damn time too.

TWO
JACE

It was too damn hot to be here, but we met at the Gilded Cage on the last Friday of every month, and after Erik's call last night, I knew I couldn't beg off. Now, sitting here at the table, I could see why. All around us, people were laughing and drinking and flirting, but the four of us looked like we were at a funeral.

Well, not *all* four of us.

The sandy-haired man sitting across from me was listening to a tale of woe, but Erik Sanders couldn't stop himself from smiling. Not because anything Alix Wexler was saying was funny or anything like that, I knew. Erik was thinking about Tanya Lacey, his *girlfriend*. Which was ironic, considering Alix was currently fucked up over a girl. His assistant, apparently. They'd had a thing, and then he just vanished. Sent him a text yesterday saying they were done. No explanation, nothing.

He should have known better. Erik might be claiming to have found his soulmate or whatever, but the rest of us knew that wasn't how things worked. After all, Reb and I both had personal experience telling us that the best we could hope for was a woman who wouldn't sell out our secrets to the media. While the perception of the BDSM lifestyle may have changed a little over the years, and those of us in any sort of artistic profession usually got a pass when it came to sexual proclivities, none of us wanted our names and faces splashed across the tabloids with stories about whips and leather.

Not that leather was my thing. Whips, on the other hand...

I looked up as a hand brushed my shoulder. A tall red-head gave me a look out of the corner of her eye, and I recognized the gleam. It wasn't like she was being subtle about it. Too many of the women who came here claiming to be subs thought they knew what they wanted because they'd read some book about alpha males and Dominants without really trying to understand the true meaning underneath it all. They thought they'd find some rich playboy who liked kinky sex and just needed the love of a good woman.

"Jace!"

I jerked my head around to find Reb giving me an

impatient look that said he'd been trying to get my attention for a while.

"What?" I took a drink of my beer and wondered if I should get something stronger.

His eyebrow shot up, a wicked look on his face. "You up for being my wingman?"

All of us got our fair share of admiration, but rock star Reb Union definitely attracted the most attention. He had that sort of charisma that drew people to him, but he never lorded it over others. It was thanks to him I'd come to be part of this group since I'd been the odd man out. Erik and Alix were cousins. And Erik and Reb had been roommates during the short time Reb was in college. I was the oldest out of the four of us, and I'd already been going to Gilded Cage for a couple years when they started coming, but I'd never made a point to talk to anyone, to make friends. I came for sex, and that had been it.

I'd been sitting by the bar when Reb sat down next to me and started complaining about the song that was playing at the time. The two of us started talking classic rock, and the rest was history.

I looked around the room. It was a Friday night in late June, so the place was packed. The dance floor was full of writhing bodies, some dressed simply like me, in jeans and a short-sleeved shirt, some in the more extreme costumes of the S&M crowd. Gilded Cage was a bit more exclusive than other BDSM clubs in that not just anyone could walk in off the street, but it still managed to be full to capacity with some of the most beautiful and sexy people in the city.

"How do you want to play this?" I asked, looking around at our options. "I'm not really in the mood for seduction tonight."

He shook his head, his eyes darkened to almost purple. "Me either. I don't want someone who wants any of that romantic shit. Just sex and for one night only."

"That makes two of us," I muttered as I stood.

I found myself scanning the crowd almost as a second thought, then caught myself. I didn't need to do that anymore. She hadn't been here in a long time. It was just times like tonight, when things got to me and everything else was going to shit, I found myself pulled to the past, even when I didn't want to be.

I needed to get my head out of my life for a while. Stop thinking so much about every damn thing. I knew that was why I hadn't been able to paint anything half decent in my studio in months. I'd start something and lose it halfway through. I had more than a dozen half-finished canvases in my studio, and absolutely no desire to work on any of them.

Reb tapped my arm and jerked his chin toward two blondes a few tables over. They looked enough alike for me to guess they were sisters. Pretty. Both wearing similar slinky dresses that clung to their curves enough for me to see that, even from where I stood, they both had pierced nipples.

The two of us fell into step together, and the crowd parted for us, the subs automatically dipping their heads, the Doms giving us nods of acknowledgement. We weren't the oldest or most prominent members, or even the wealthiest – which was saying something – but we'd made a name for ourselves among the BDSM crowd.

That was something.

And it was enough to get one of the blondes – she gave her name as Lillian – to come back with me to one of the VIP rooms.

Less than fifteen minutes later, she was bent over a padded bench, her arms stretched out on either side, soft leather cuffs around her wrists to hold her in place. Her breasts hung over the front as well, and I'd fastened a pair of weights to both of the silver rings in each nipple, stretching them. She made the most delicious sounds as I followed through on what I promised to do to her.

Her ankles were attached to a spreader bar, forcing her legs far apart enough to let me see how wet her pussy was. Not that I needed to see it when I could feel it with the three fingers I was currently working in and out of her. Her muscles tensed and bunched as she tried to push back against my hand, but I'd secured her tightly enough that she couldn't move.

"Are you close?" I asked as I rubbed my thumb against her clit.

"Yes," she breathed, the word coming out between harsh pants. "I need more."

I waited a few more seconds, then removed my hand. She made a noise of protest but didn't say anything as I stood. We'd taken a couple minutes to set limits before we got started, so I knew I could push her, and that was exactly what I was craving at the moment. The rush that came with the absolute control over a person's pain and pleasure. I didn't need to wait for inspiration to strike, or worry about losing focus half-way through. This was something I could do, and I did it well.

I knew the options the club presented for its members, so I'd already been choosing my preferred...*instruments* even as we walked back to the room. I crossed to the far wall and picked up a thin riding crop. Lillian had been open about her masochistic tendencies, so I knew this was a better choice than the softer flogger or cat o'nine tails I would have used on a less experienced sub. I could see the appeal of taking a blank slate, but there were definitely benefits of being with someone who knew her desires were in line with mine.

As I moved back to stand behind her again, I had a moment where it hit me with sudden clarity that all of this was utterly pointless. That the search for control, for pain and pleasure, for dominance and submission, all of it, didn't mean a thing without the deep connection Erik had found.

I shook the thought off almost as soon as it came. I wasn't looking for any of that. I'd tried it before and it hadn't worked. It never worked. I really hoped Erik and Tanya beat the odds, but if anything, what happened between Alix and Sine was proof that it didn't matter how intense a connection felt. It never lasted. And if it couldn't last, what was the point of trying to force something deeper than it should go?

I tapped the end of the crop against the base of her spine, then traced a line down one butt cheek, then the other, letting her prepare herself for what was coming. I would leave red stripes on her tanned flesh, enough for her to feel them for the weekend. I'd use the crop on her pussy and her clit, not hard enough to damage her, but she'd be whimpering by the time I finished. I'd take her right to the edge of her pain threshold, and then I would fuck her, let the pain mingle with pleasure until she came and came, until she screamed my name.

And I'd find my own release, not only physically but mentally as well.

I was using her, I knew, but she was using me too, and that was fine. It had to be. Because there wasn't anything else.

THREE
SAVANNAH

Everett looked too damn chipper considering how little sleep he must have gotten last night. He and his boy-toy had been loudly enthusiastic pretty much until dawn. I'd gone out to do some errands before the heat got too overwhelming, so I missed the morning after show, but I'd seen enough of them over the years to know how it went.

"I still don't get why you like this shit," Everett said as he set my drink in front of me. "I mean, Iced Chestnut Praline Latte? What the hell is that supposed to be, anyway?"

"Delicious and much-needed sugar and caffeine," I said matter-of-factly, then practically inhaled a mouthful. "Thank you."

"I heard your boy leaving just after midnight. Seems to me you got plenty of sleep," Everett said.

I glared at him even as a few women passed behind him, clearly checking him out. He really was too attractive for his own good.

"I *would* have gotten sleep if someone hadn't been making wild monkey love at all hours," I pointed out.

To my surprise, he flushed, then pointed at the plate in front of me. "Eat your Gaeng Keow Wan."

I raised an eyebrow and took a couple bites of my favorite Thai meal. It said a lot about how well the two of us knew each other that he knew exactly what I ordered even though I'd placed the orders while he'd gone to get us drinks at the coffee place next door. We'd been coming here often enough over the last couple years that the owners didn't mind if we snuck in drinks from time to time.

After a few minutes of eating in silence, he asked, "So was that guy not that good? I mean, you certainly weren't howling with pleasure."

I rolled my eyes, but there was no embarrassment. The two of us had gotten past any of that ages ago. We shared everything. Hopes. Dreams. Nightmares. Problems. Struggles. Sex. Love. No subject was taboo. Everett had said more than once that we were true soulmates, two parts of a single whole.

And without the fuck-ups that sex usually brought to a relationship.

"Come on, Sav," he continued, reaching across the table to steal a forkful of curry chicken. "Seriously. When was the last time a guy stay all night because once just wasn't enough?"

I was about to give him a sarcastic response when it hit me. I couldn't remember. And it wasn't that I couldn't remember the last time a guy had been so good that I wanted more. I couldn't remember the last time I'd wanted to fall asleep in a guy's arms. Not just wanted to, but hadn't been able to help myself.

"He wasn't bad," I said finally. "I mean, he managed to get me off, which is better than some of the other guys I've fucked."

Everett's expression sobered. "Is that really what you want? A guy that's just 'not bad' or just better than someone else?"

I raised an eyebrow as I took the last couple bites of my meal, and then I countered his questions with my own. "Isn't that what hooking up is essentially? Finding someone to fuck who was halfway decent?"

He shrugged and looked down at his cup. Poked at his Goong Chu Chee.

"Ev?"

He sighed and raised his head. "I'm thinking that maybe I want something more."

"Really?" I didn't bother to hide my surprise. "You sounded like you were having plenty of fun last night."

"I did," he admitted, his fingers shredding his napkin. To my continued amazement, his cheeks stained red. "And

I asked Cal if he wanted to go out tonight. Like on a real date."

"His name is Cal?" I leaned forward and covered his hand with mine, a big grin spreading across my face. "From the way you were yelling, I thought his name was *oh fuck me harder*."

"Bitch," Everett muttered good naturedly, a smile playing on his lips.

I laughed and tossed a balled-up napkin at him. "Seriously though, if that's what you want, good for you."

"But that's not what you want?"

I leaned back in my seat and shook my head. "Come on, Ev, you know me better than that. Besides, with my new assignment starting tomorrow, I have enough to focus on."

"That's right," he said, his eyes lighting up. "I want details about this artist you've been gushing about."

"You'll have them as soon as I do," I promised. "But I doubt it'll be anything as exciting as your *fuck me harder Cal*."

His returned lob of my napkin hit me square in the forehead.

FOUR
JACE

"Fuck!" I shouted as I tossed my paintbrush at the canvas. It left a smear of deep maroon across what had been a sea of blue.

I'd spent nearly two hours with Lillian on Friday night, and by the time we parted ways, we'd both been sated. Physically, at least. But the turmoil in my mind hadn't truly calmed. On the surface, I'd had some peace – enough to sleep – but when I woke up on Saturday and tried to sketch out a new picture to paint, the paper remained blank.

By evening, I'd resigned myself to failure. Again. I picked up a book on Monet and managed to lose myself for a few hours. Yesterday, I hadn't even bothered to try. I sat in the dark and shadowed living room, staring at a TV I didn't really see, and wondered how I'd lost the thing that had always been my safe haven.

I could still remember the first time I picked up a paintbrush. I was six years-old, and Mom and I had gone to a mission on Christmas Eve because we barely had enough money to keep the lights on, so presents had been out of the question. We hadn't even had a tree. We'd hung lights and ornaments on coat hangers, and pretended it was a game. But Mom had said she wanted me to have at least one gift, so she walked up to one of the women there and asked where the gifts were...for teenage girls. Because she had a daughter who was still at work, and she wanted to get gifts for both of us.

I'd watched my mom eagerly pick through the choices until she'd found a manicure set, complete with nail polish and fake nails. Then she glanced over at me, walked over to another table, grabbed the first thing she saw and shoved it at me. As we walked away, I remember wondering if I should have told the lady that I didn't have a sister. Then I'd looked down at the box my mom handed me, and it had been like everything else disappeared.

It had been an introductory art set. And not just simple watercolors that would've been appropriate for a child my age. It had watercolors, finger paints, and a couple tubes of more expensive water and oil based paints. There'd also been different brushes and sponges, a few sketching pencils, charcoal pencils, and even a palate knife. And the sculpting clay that even now I tried to forget.

It hadn't been until I was in my teens that I realized someone had spent a lot of money putting that box together. I even tried to find out, but I'd never been able to learn who had been responsible for saving my life.

Because that's what happened. As my mother had spent more and more time with her various boyfriends, I'd lost myself in the world of colors and textures. I didn't just love how the colors played off each other. I loved how different techniques could give the identical picture a completely new look and meaning.

When I'd been picked up by Child Protective Services after spending a month and a half by myself at the age of ten, painting had been my solace. When my mother had come with a man she'd introduced as my father, I'd expressed myself through art. When my father sent me to boarding school because he hadn't known how to handle having a child, painting had come with me. When he'd had a stroke in the middle of my senior year of high school and had lingered in the eight years that followed, art had been my salvation.

It was the one thing in my life I'd been able to count on. It had never abandoned me...until now.

"Son of a bitch," I muttered as I kicked at a crumpled paper towel. The still-wet paint on it left a smudge of green on my bare foot. I'd been trying to create something with the paper towel as a medium, but I'd lost the vision partway through, just like I had with everything else.

It had never been this hard. Not in this way. It was work, like all art, and anyone who said otherwise either didn't know what the hell they were talking about, or they'd never seen anyone who'd created anything of quality. I'd heard someone once compare art to exercise. No matter how much you loved it, and how much natural ability you had, it still needed blood, sweat, and tears if it was going to be any good.

But it had never been like this before.

Like I was reaching deep inside me for something that had always been there, and I'd come up empty. Even the desire to create was waning, and with its loss came the fear that it would never return. That I would lose this refuge.

I was thirty-three years-old and hadn't needed to worry about money from the moment Benjamin Gooding accepted me as his son. I was his only heir, so I'd been in control of his massive estate since his stroke. When he finally passed, I inherited it all, including a villa in the south of France, a share in a Napa Valley winery, a house in the Hamptons, and the family mansion on the Upper East Side, which was where I lived most of the time.

Even though it was far too large for just me, I kept it because I knew how important family had been to my father. We hadn't been close, and I'd been a handful, but he never made me feel like a burden, not even when I spent a couple years in boarding school. By the time I was sixteen, he turned half of the first floor into a studio for me, putting in massive windows to allow in as much natural light as possible. He also added a private entrance and private staircase to the third floor so that I could come and go as I pleased without worrying about disturbing him.

I scratched my head as I wandered over to one of the floor-to-ceiling windows. Maybe the problem was that I needed to get out of the city. I could go to the Hamptons for a while. I had a smaller studio there. Or maybe I needed to get away from the East Coast all together. My friends and I shared a house in Aspen that might be just what I needed. Mountains could give me a new perspective.

Except I knew the problem had nothing to do with where I was. It was me. I was off-balance, as if the axis of my world had somehow shifted without me knowing it and everything was off-kilter.

I'd read somewhere that a true explorer might use a compass, but that he also knew how to navigate using the stars. There were things that could throw off a compass's ability to find true north, but if a person studied the stars and their places in the sky, he could never really be lost.

And that's what it felt like, I realized. Like I'd spent my

whole life using a compass to find direction and had never bothered to learn any other way, so when something had come along to mess with it, I wasn't able to regain my footing.

I needed to look to the stars.

The idea of constellations and planets whirled through my head, as if searching for some spark of life, of creativity, to give it form. It was right there, just out of my grasp, and I knew there was some essential part that hadn't quite clicked into place. A part that was necessary before I could see the big picture.

I was still musing over it when the sound of the doorbell interrupted my thoughts. I'd ordered lunch from my favorite restaurant and asked them to bring it to the private entrance, so I didn't bother looking to see who was there. The moment I opened the door, I wondered why the hell someone who looked like *that* was delivering my samosa and chicken tandoori.

She was just a couple inches over five feet tall and slender, with the sort of delicate features that immediately made me feel like someone should be protecting her rather than letting her wander around the city by herself. She wore a simple steel gray blouse and a plain black skirt that seemed way too fancy for such a mundane job. Her rich, sepia brown hair was pulled back from her face, with a couple escaping curls that I was far too tempted to twist around my finger just to see if it was as silky as it looked. Her eyes were an extraordinary light gray that reminded me of pure, pale ash that could almost be mistaken for snow.

Well, damn.

FIVE
SAVANNAH

I'd been so nervous about my first real assignment that I barely slept at all. By five o'clock, I'd known it was completely useless to stay in bed, so I'd gotten up and gone for a run. I wasn't a runner by nature, but it was as good a way as any to work off stress and clear my mind.

By the time I was showered and had gone through every outfit in my closet, and even a couple of Everett's shirts, my nerves were back, but they were at least manageable.

"I like it," Everett said as I walked into the kitchen. "But you might want to put on a bra under that shirt. Unless your plan is to let Jace Randell see your nipples on the first day."

I stopped, mouth hanging open, then ran into the bathroom. Shit. He was right. I'd forgotten to put on a bra, and this blouse was so thin that without it, my nipples would be pointing at everyone who saw me.

I was still flustered when I sat down at the table, and the fact that Everett was smirking didn't help matters much. I couldn't eat but a few bites no matter how delicious the French toast was that Everett had made.

"Don't you have to be at work soon?" I snapped, the words coming out harsher than I intended.

He kept grinning. "Day off."

I glared at him and managed to eat another bite of food. Everett already had his BS in applied physics, but was currently working on his Masters. He was also a maintenance worker in the NYU physics department, but I was fairly certain he spent most of his time flirting with any guy who caught his eye.

His antics, however, did manage to take the edge off my nerves, so as I got out of the cab on 69th Street, I finally felt like I could handle this. After all, I'd gone to school for this. A journalism degree from NYU with a minor in art history, all with the intention of becoming an art critic – every minute of study had been pointing toward this moment.

I'd worked my ass off on all the shitty assignments my boss gave me over the past eighteen months, pretty much all of which involved proofreading and fact gathering for the pretentious puff pieces he wrote. Through it all, I kept my eye on the prize. *This* prize.

I took a slow breath and made my way up the sidewalk. I'd been told to use a side door, so I bypassed the front and rang the doorbell. As I waited for someone to answer, I mentally prepared myself to meet the artist whose work had inspired my career.

I was a junior in high school when our art teacher had taken my class to Indianapolis to see a gallery his sister had just opened. In it, there were three pieces by a brand new artist. I must have stood there for two hours, looking at them in turn, and then back again. I'd written my senior thesis about them and gotten a near-perfect grade.

Then the door opened and...well, damn.

I'd seen pictures of him, but they'd clearly all been staged, because while he looked good in a suit and tie, *this* was clearly the true artist.

Ash blond hair possessed little streaks of maroon that matched the flecks on the tight black shirt that showed off the amazing definition his suit jackets had hidden. Jade green eyes and hints of tattoos peeked out from under his short sleeves. His long legs were covered by a pair of paint-stained jeans that I didn't even want to see from behind because I just *knew* they'd hug the tightest ass I'd ever seen.

"How much?"

My eyebrows shot up. Well, that was one way to keep me from ogling him. "Excuse me?"

He gave me an odd look and ran his hand through his

hair, answering the question of how he'd gotten paint highlighted through the strands. "How much do I owe you?" His gaze darted down to my hands, then back up. "Did you forget the food?"

Now it was my turn to give him a strange look. "What are you talking about?"

His mouth curved into a half-smile. "You're not here to deliver my lunch, are you?"

I chuckled and tried to hide how thrown – and charmed – I was. "I think we have a miscommunication." I held out my hand. "I'm Savannah Birch, the reporter slash critic from *The Heart of Art*."

I silently congratulated myself for not making a face at the magazine's name. They hired me and a couple other writers in their early twenties to try to revitalize their image, but they still had a way to go.

His half-smile fell into a sardonic one as he reached out to clasp my hand. I swallowed a gasp at the heat and electricity that flowed out from where his skin touched mine. I mean, I knew he was hot. I had eyes. But that connection, it was beyond attraction. It was like an almost audible click.

"Come in," he said as he took a step back out of the doorway. "I was just getting ready to break for lunch."

As I stepped past him, I caught his scent – paint and soap and some underlying masculine smell that twisted primal things low in my stomach. Shit. I could get addicted to that.

"Sorry about how that sounded," he said. "Me asking how much. I promise that I meant it in the most innocent way possible."

With a voice like that, I doubted anything he ever said could be construed as innocent. I could get wet just listening to him read an owner's manual.

"A simple misunderstanding," I said with what I hoped was a professional smile. I definitely didn't want him to know how attractive I thought he was. The last thing I needed was my first relevant assignment to go up in smoke because I couldn't keep my hormones under control.

He was gorgeous. Big deal. I'd already prepared myself to deal with some level of hero worship. Some physical attraction on top of that shouldn't be an issue. I'd never let it be one before. I mean, my best friend was hot, and it'd never been an issue between us. Sure, he was gay, but plenty of straight women had crushes on gay guys.

That was what I needed to do. Pretend Jace was gay. Because then it wouldn't matter that his ass was even better than I thought it would be, or that I'd suddenly fixated on his hands. Those long, strong fingers. Fuck. I shivered at the thought of the things those fingers could do.

How they would feel on my body. Inside me. If they would caress my breasts or be rough and pinch my nipples until they throbbed. If he'd wrap those fingers around my wrists and hold them, restrain me...

Fuck.

I closed my eyes for a moment and ran through a list of my favorite artists by year and categorization. Anything that would keep me from thinking about what it would be like to have those artist's hands...

Shit.

"Ms. Birch? Are you all right?"

I opened my eyes and forced a smile as I turned. "I'm fine, thank you."

Before I could say anything else, the doorbell rang again.

"That probably *is* my food this time," he said as he stepped around me. "I'll be right back. Make yourself comfortable."

As he walked back the way we'd come, I forced myself to turn away before I could start picturing the way that ass would look bare. The muscles tensing as he pumped...

"Fuck," I muttered.

It shouldn't have been this difficult to get my mind out of the gutter. I'd never been a flighty person, distracted by a pretty face or a nice body. I was driven by my work.

And I didn't date artists. Hell, as long as I could help it, I didn't even *fuck* artists. Most creative people tended to be on the...temperamental side. Which meant emotional. Dramatic. Yes, passionate, but I had no problem giving up a bit of passion if it meant I didn't have to deal with any drama. Women generally had the reputation of being the ones who freaked out about sex, but I believed in equal opportunities for everyone when it came to making fools of themselves.

Which meant, when it came to sex, I drew a firm line in the sand, and I wasn't going to cross it.

Not even for someone as amazing as Jace Randell.

SIX
JACE

I didn't think I'd ever met anyone quite like Savannah Birch. Sure, I'd met beautiful women, delicate women. What I'd never seen was a woman who had been insulted take it so well. The moment I realized that she wasn't delivering my food, I realized that my having asked her *how much* could have been taken in a very non-food way. Any other woman who thought she'd been mistaken for a prostitute would have been insulted. Well, most women anyway, and the ones with class *definitely*, and she certainly had class.

She hadn't demanded an apology, even though it had technically just been a misunderstanding, and I appreciated that. Then she'd introduced herself, and I realized she knew who I was. And she hadn't hit on me.

I wasn't an arrogant person, but I *was* self-aware enough to know that based on looks alone, most women would have, at the very least, been flirting with me. I was also not naive enough to think that once someone discovered just how much money I had, that they wouldn't want me for that alone. So the fact that Savannah hadn't acted on any of the desire I'd seen in her eyes spoke volumes about either her self-control, or her dedication to her job.

Or I'd completely misread the fact that she wanted me.

I walked back into the studio with my food. As was all too often my habit when I was working, I ordered way more than I'd be able to eat in one sitting so I wouldn't have to worry about interrupting the flow to order again. I supposed a part of me was hoping that following my normal routine for creating would trigger something.

It hadn't, but at least I now had enough food to offer my guest.

"Sorry," I apologized as I took the food over to the small table I used when I was too caught up in what I was doing to leave the studio. "I hadn't realized you were coming, or I would have gotten us something nicer for lunch. I have enough to share if you like Indian food."

She gave me a puzzled look that wasn't quite fast enough to cover the flare of heat I'd seen hidden behind her unique irises. Any previous doubt I'd had about whether or not she was attracted to me disappeared, and it surprised me that I actually cared.

"No one told you I was coming?"

I gestured toward one of the other chairs as I sat down. "No. Was someone supposed to?"

She frowned, but she seemed to be more confused than annoyed. "I thought they were."

"Sit," I said, nodding to the chair across from me. "Eat."

To my surprise, she took the seat closest to me, close enough that when she crossed her legs, the toes of her shoe brushed my knee. She picked up one of the cartons, gave it a serious look, then picked up a fork and took a couple bites.

Maybe it'd been too long since I'd been on an actual date because I found myself staring at her while she ate. Partly, I was watching her mouth because she had these amazing lips. A perfect cupid's bow at the top, and a bottom lip a little fuller, but not so plump that her mouth looked unbalanced.

While her looks were captivating, another part of me was more fascinated that she had no qualms about eating in front of me. My ex had refused to eat more than a few bites in my presence, as if I'd ever said a word about her weight or what she ate. As an artist, I was not only a firm believer that beauty came in all shapes and sizes, I actually didn't have one particular body type that appealed over another.

"Is something wrong?"

It took her question to make me realize that I'd stopped eating and was staring at her.

"Sorry." I gave myself a mental shake and refocused on my food. "I was just thinking about what you said about someone calling me."

I reached over to the small refrigerator and took out two bottles of water. I handed one to her and opened the other for myself. I had a couple bottles of beer in there too, but I rarely imbibed when I was trying to work. I knew some artists felt like alcohol enhanced their creativity, but that wasn't the case for me. I generally only indulged if I was tensed up from not being able to paint, but something about Savannah made me think having a clear head would be best.

"My boss assigned me to cover the show you have coming up." She took a long drink of her water. "He said I should stop by today to meet with you, get some backstory, find out why you were finally doing interviews. I assumed that meant he talked to someone – you or your agent or whatever – but apparently, I should have asked."

"Don't worry about it." I almost told her that I hadn't actually accomplished anything before she arrived, but then figured that, as intrigued as I was by her, it still wouldn't be smart to share *that* particular bit of information with a journalist I didn't know.

"So, do you have a few minutes to spare for some questions?"

Her question wasn't timid, but it also wasn't pushy. She managed to find that balance that most people in the media didn't have. It was a good quality for an art critic, being able to extract information from the upper crust of society without them feeling pressured.

"It's fine if you can't," she added and set a mostly empty carton back on the table. "I'll schedule a meeting for another day."

I shook my head. "I have time." I finished off my bottle of water as I waited for her to begin.

Except she didn't.

A flush crept up her cheeks, and I wondered if it was because she didn't know what to say...or because she was thinking something entirely inappropriate. Despite not being interested in a relationship, and having absolutely no intention of getting involved with a reporter even for a single night, I couldn't help hoping it was the latter of the two. I didn't usually find myself wanting a woman to be attracted to me, but my instincts continued to tell me that she was no ordinary woman.

It took approximately a minute and a half for my curiosity about her to overcome my patience.

"So, are you a fan of art, or is this a story you were assigned at random?"

She raised her head, her jaw taking on a stubborn set. "I have a degree in journalism with a minor in art history from NYU. I want to be an art critic."

One corner of my mouth quirked up before I could stop it. "Good to know. Most reporters I talk to consider an art piece to be just a step or two above covering a garden show. Working for a magazine like *The Heart of Art* wouldn't be much better than doing fluff entertainment pieces in their eyes."

"It's all I've wanted to do since I first saw–" She stopped suddenly, even more color flooding her face. She took a slow breath, and then went on, "When I was a junior in high school, I went on a trip to an art gallery and saw three paintings that changed my life. I don't have any artistic talent, but at that moment, I knew that I had to find a place in that world."

The first thing that hit me was the intensity and passion I could see in her eyes, hear in her words. The second was that she appeared to gain confidence as she gave me that insight into her life.

"What paintings?" I asked, unconsciously leaning forward. If they had inspired something so genuine in this woman, perhaps they could do the same for me.

Something strange flickered in her eyes, as if she had to make some sort of decision about what she said next, but then she squared her shoulders and answered my question. "*A Spirit in the Woods*, *A Maiden's Regret*, and *Tempestuous Stars*."

It was my turn to be speechless for several seconds. Those were *my* paintings. If I'd given them no name at all or something a bit more common, then I might have thought it was a coincidence, that she'd happened to see some paintings that shared the titles of mine, but the odds were too high for it to be anything else.

"Where did you see those?" The question was completely inane, but I couldn't quite think of anything else to say yet.

"Indianapolis." I felt her assessing me from under her lashes. "You'd just sold them to the owner of the gallery. Her brother was my art teacher."

I remembered that, I realized with a start. They were the first pieces I'd ever sold, and I made the connection through one of the nurses who helped look after my father those last few years. I'd wanted to celebrate, but there hadn't been anyone I could think of to call or tell who would actually care. It was the same night I found Gilded Cage.

Fate and destiny weren't words I generally used, but I couldn't deny how serendipitous it felt that the same three paintings that had brought me to my friends and to a world where my preferences were considered normal, had also connected me with a woman I couldn't help but want to get to know.

"If you were a junior then, it would make you..." I let the question trail off and hoped she wouldn't be offended that I was fishing for her age. I originally thought she was probably still in college, but now I was putting her a bit older than that.

"Twenty-five." She grinned, causing those unique eyes to almost sparkle. "Though I've heard it's not polite to ask a lady her age."

Her grin was contagious, and I found myself smiling back.

"So, my paintings made you decide to become an art critic? I'm trying to decide if that's a good or bad thing."

"Good." She laughed, a sweet, husky sound that rolled over me with the sort of sensuality I couldn't ignore. "I'd always liked art, but when I saw them...they spoke to something in me. The way you worked varying textures into the different colors so that the contrasts were more than between the various shades. They made me want to add touch to sight, to give blue a specific feel against my fingertips."

As she talked, a feeling uncoiled in my chest, something I couldn't identify at first, but then realized was...love. I'd been painting for release, for an outlet, and because I had a show I needed new work for, but it had been a long time since I'd painted simply for the joy of it. And that was what I wanted to do now. I wanted to go back to my canvases and paint because before, even when it had been an outlet for me, I once loved it. Somewhere along the way, I lost that. Listening to Savannah talk about the different pieces I'd created and how they made her feel brought that desire back again.

For the first time in months, maybe longer, I thought that I might be able to paint again. It might not yield anything worth a gallery, but it would set me on the road back to where I wanted to be.

For a number of reasons, I was suddenly very glad that Savannah's editor had sent her my way.

SEVEN
SAVANNAH

I hadn't planned on discussing my personal experience with his art. I hadn't planned on discussing anything of a personal nature, actually, and certainly not on my end of things. This was supposed to be about him, about his show, but he completely disarmed me. He was nothing like I expected. I hadn't read anything negative about him, so it hadn't been like I'd walked in the door thinking he was this playboy partier or anything like that. His past wasn't well-known, and I hadn't tried to dig into it because this was supposed to be about his art.

I told myself this was why I was so enthusiastically describing the way his work made me feel, how I saw it. It had nothing to do with the need to tell the person who'd opened my eyes to the world in a new way just what he'd done for me.

It wasn't until I finally stopped talking that I realized I'd been going on for nearly five solid minutes while he just sat there and listened. Not for the first time today, my face was red.

"Thank you." His tone was sincere, his eyes kind.

And yet, under that kindness was a heat that spoke to me in a different way.

A way I wanted to ignore, even as I wanted to embrace it.

"Sorry about that." I gave him a rueful smile. "When I got the assignment, I told myself I wouldn't do that."

He smiled, leaning toward me. "It's been a long time since I've seen someone be that passionate about art – any art – let alone mine. Most of the people I talk to have all sorts of pretentious words they like to use, but not a single one of them mean anything."

A moment settled between us, and I knew it could turn so many different ways. Awkward as we realized we'd gone a step too far toward personal. Romantic as we gave in to the connection I knew was between us. Or I could make sure things went the way they were supposed to go. The way they should have gone from the beginning.

"Art is important to me." I hoped my smile was more professional than it felt. "And I believe that yours is exceptional."

"I thought an art critic wasn't supposed to come in with

any biases." He sounded like he was teasing, but I could tell we were back on solid ground.

I laughed. "If college taught me anything, it's that no one goes into any sort of review or critique without any biases."

He leaned back in his chair, everything about his body language more relaxed than it had been. "Where do you want to start?"

"Can you tell me a bit about the show that's coming up?" I set down a small notepad on the table. "Like why you chose this particular event."

"It's a great charity." There wasn't a trace of deceit or self-satisfaction in his voice. "Clean drinking water is more important than most people realize, and if I can help raise money by talking to a reporter and donating some art, I'm glad to help."

"There doesn't seem to be much in the way of details of what's going to be shown."

A shadow seemed to settle over him, and he shrugged, but I could still see something negative lingering there.

"We haven't really decided on a theme," he said finally. "A way to present the work. There's nothing really...clear about it."

I nodded, knowing it wouldn't do any good to push at the moment. "Okay. Let's shift away from your work then. You don't really do many interviews, and the ones you have done don't really talk much about your art."

He shifted uncomfortably. "Most reporters are more interested in my bank balance and my family connections than they are in art."

"Well, I'm not most reporters." I hoped he didn't paint me with the same brush as my peers – pun intended. "If you want to talk about how your bank balance and your family connections affect your art, you're more than welcome to, but otherwise, I'm not planning on writing anything about either of those subjects."

He tilted his head, eyes narrowing as if he was studying me. "So you want to know about my influences? Want me to say how I studied the greats like da Vinci and van Gogh? Or maybe one of those new controversial artists who like to smear shit on things that everyone thinks are important and call it making a statement?"

His questions weren't angry, but I caught a definite edge to them, as if they were a test rather than rhetorical. I wasn't sure what he was waiting to hear, but I gave him the truth.

"I've never been one of those people who thinks that the popularity of a particular artist or subject is what makes it quality. Most of the ones who use sensationalism to sell their work don't actually have any talent." I tapped my pen on the notebook. "But I also don't think that, just because something is popular, it isn't any good either. I judge purely on the art itself."

He nodded as if I'd said something right. "All right then, let's talk artistic influences."

The next thing I knew, almost two hours had passed. Jace answered all of my questions, but it had been more than an interview. Even though we kept our conversation completely professional, there had been an undercurrent I couldn't deny.

When his phone rang, a part of me was actually relieved. I admired him as an artist, and I wanted to write my best work so that others could see how amazing he was as much as I did for my own benefit. I didn't want to do anything that could screw it up.

I gave him a brief wave as I stood, silently letting him know that I would see myself out. He nodded and smiled, then turned his back on me, stepping out of the kitchen. I felt a mild pang of jealousy as I wondered if he was talking to his girlfriend. He hadn't said anything about his romantic life, but all that meant was that he was good at keeping things quiet.

I put my notebook back into my purse, then figured the least I could do since he bought me dinner would be to clean up a bit. I tossed the empty cartons and bottles into the trash, then opened the fridge to put the leftovers away. As I closed it and turned away, out of the corner of my eye, I saw something fall. I picked it up and realized it was a matchbook, the sort that some hotels and clubs still passed out for advertising.

It was plain and black, with two words written in fancy script.

Gilded Cage.

I'd never heard of it, and I had no reason to think that I'd be interested in whatever club or hotel this matchbook was from, but I still slipped it in my pocket. If it was a club, maybe it was worth checking out. Everett would probably be game, even if it was a straight club. If it was a gay one, that might be what I needed too: to find out that Jace was gay. That would make it a whole lot easier to just admire his looks and not keep thinking about what it would be like to feel his hands all over my body, his mouth moving down...

Shit.

I needed to go home and get a cold shower. Now.

"WHAT DO you mean you didn't see the paintings for the show?"

I tried not to flinch as spittle flew from my boss's lips and showered the top of his desk. I wasn't the kind of person who judged others by how they looked, but when a person's actions made them into a pervert, it did tend to influence how I saw their appearance. Thinning brown hair, wire-rimmed glasses, and an extra hundred fifty pounds on a six-foot frame – none of those things would've screamed *please keep your hands off me,* but the lecherous look in those dark eyes of his...yeah, those made me do everything in my power to keep at least one piece of furniture between Abel Updike and myself.

"I got backstory today," I said, keeping my voice even. "I'll speak to Mr. Randall in a day or two about a private showing so I can get an impression of the paintings on their own, then I'll attend the show to see how they look in the space."

Abel rolled his eyes and leaned back. The chair creaked in protest, and I waited to see if, this time, it would give up the ghost. "When I did my doctorate thesis..."

I tuned him out. I wasn't trying to be rude, I'd just heard this speech before. At least a dozen times before. He'd talk about how he did his doctorate thesis on artists in the French Renaissance, neglecting to mention that the online school where he'd gotten his Ph.D. had since gone belly up. Once he explained the topic in the most possible condescending tone possible, he'd continue on for another quarter of an hour or so about how he'd write all of the copy if he could, but he was so busy that it wasn't possible and blah, blah, blah.

I let him go through it all again while I mentally went through the contents of my closet. When I got home last night, I texted my friends about Gilded Cage, but none of them had ever heard of it, and even if they had, they wouldn't have been able to go with me until the weekend.

It *was* a club. I might have focused on being an art critic, but I knew how to investigate. I didn't know what type of club it was, but I managed to find an address. Now, I was thinking I might take a trip tonight just as something to do to get my mind off of how much I wished I could tell Abel exactly what I thought of him.

And if I happened to see a handsome artist there, I might feel obligated to have a dance or two with him.

Purely out of politeness, of course.

EIGHT
SAVANNAH

Not knowing what sort of club Gilded Cage was, I'd gone with the ever classic little black dress. It was an off-the-shoulder slinky number I usually wore without a bra. I'd forgone jewelry and kept the makeup and hair simple, but had chosen a pair of heels that added nearly five inches to my height and made my legs look amazing.

I'd suspected that the club was a private one, but as I watched from across the street, I began to think that it wasn't merely private, but elite, the sort of place where one needed a sponsor of some kind to be granted access. Fortunately for me, I had the name of someone I believed was a member. I just hoped using it wouldn't prove to be as stupid as I expected it would be.

I smiled up at the man who blocked my entrance and resisted the urge to press my hands against my skirt to dry my palms. When it came to getting into restricted places, confidence could go a long way. "I'm meeting Jace Randall here."

His eyes moved over me, but not in a sexual way, more like if he was trying to see if I matched the sort of woman Jace would normally bring to something like this. He nodded once. "Is he bringing your mask?"

Shit. I hadn't considered that it might be a place that required masks. What had I gotten myself into?

"We have extras inside," he continued. "In case anyone forgot that tonight was a masquerade."

I pushed the sudden influx of nerves away. "Thank you. Jace must have forgotten. Busy with his upcoming show."

I kept the smile as I walked past him, my eyes widening as I stepped closer to the tables with masks, not just simple ones, but ones elaborate enough to cover most of my face and prevent Jace from recognizing me if he showed up. While a part of me wanted to see him here, another part didn't want him to know that I'd stolen the matches with the sole purpose of finding Gilded Cage. He might think I was stalking him.

When I reached the section of the table with masks that would best fit me, I selected a one made of gold filigree and red lace. It arched over my eyebrows, then cut down on both sides to curve along my cheeks before moving back up to meet just across the bridge of my nose. It left my eyes revealed, and framed my mouth, but covered the rest of my facial features.

Perfect.

I donned the mask, checked in the mirror to make sure my hair was still good and that my face was hidden, then crossed over to the far door. As I stepped inside, the first thing that hit me was the beauty. The room was simple but elegant, all the lines and curves designed for sensuality and a natural sort of beauty. The second thing that hit me was the music. It was deep and throbbing, but not pulse-pounding club music I expected. Perhaps it was because I'd come on a theme night, but it didn't seem to have the right beat for energetic movement. No, it was the kind of music that made people want to writhe against each other, the sort of decadence that confirmed my opinion that this wasn't an ordinary elite club.

And that was when my brain finally registered the people.

Some of the women wore dresses similar to mine, sexy but nothing overtly revealing. Many of the men were in suits and tuxes. Others, however, both male and female alike, wore a whole lot less. Still, it wasn't until I saw a statuesque blonde wearing a dress made of what looked like loosely linked gold chainmail, holding a leash connected to a dark, voluptuous beauty wearing only a pair of silver studs in her nipples and what appeared to be a silver chastity belt, that it truly registered.

Shit.

This was an S&M club.

Okay, so not exactly what I'd been expecting, but it wasn't entirely shocking once I wrapped my head around it. A lot of people in the arts tended to have more liberal views toward sex, and even among the general populous, sex clubs of all kinds had been working toward more widespread acceptance over the past few years.

Even as I thought those things, I knew none of it would have made a difference to the curiosity that kept me observing rather than quickly excusing myself. I was self-aware enough to know that it wasn't simply a dispassionate interest either. From articles I'd read, I already had the inkling that this might be the type of lifestyle I'd find interesting, but it wasn't until now that I'd felt a true pull toward this world I didn't quite understand.

I was still standing on the fringes of the crowd when I felt someone watching me. It wasn't the sort of prickling feeling that came with unwanted attention, but rather a sort of heated knowing, a mental caress. I scanned the crowd, skipping over the costumes and accessories as I searched for the eyes that were on me.

He was standing only a few yards away, leaning against the bar as he sipped a drink and stared. The dim lighting made it impossible to see a specific color for his dark eyes, but nothing could have disguised the intensity in his gaze. He wore all black, including the mask that began just above his eyebrows and descended over his cheekbones to cover almost his entire face. His was cut so that the sides framed his nose and mouth while highlighting his strong, clean-shaven jaw. It didn't matter that I couldn't really see what he looked like. The compulsion I felt as I started to walk toward him had less to do with physical appearance and more to do with the sheer power I felt radiating out from him. I might not have experience in this lifestyle, but even I knew immediately that he was what they called a Dominant. He couldn't have been anything else.

He let me take half a dozen steps in his direction before he pushed away from the bar and started toward me. His long-sleeved shirt and pants were flawlessly tailored to show off the strength of his body without hindering his movements, and I wondered if he'd had those clothes made exclusively for this place, or if he wore them elsewhere.

I wasn't the only one affected by him. People parted in front of him, half of them dipping their heads as if they couldn't bear to look directly his way. I knew it was some submissive trait, but the effect was a little disconcerting. When he stopped less than a foot in front of me, he didn't say a word, but rather simply looked down at me, as if waiting to see what I would do next.

"Hi."

That wouldn't make an impression. The only thing

worse would have been if I'd asked him if he came here often.

I felt a strong and sudden longing for my friends, but it vanished almost as quickly as it came. As much as their support would have been appreciated, I wasn't going to deny that I was actually a little glad they weren't here to caution me away from the things I really hoped this man would ask me to do.

He held out a hand. "Dance?"

His voice slid over my skin, warm and heavy, barely loud enough for me to hear over the music. I didn't need to have a conversation with him to know that I wanted to dance. Hell, I wanted to do anything that let me be closer to him.

When I put my hand in his, a pleasant shiver ran through me, and I let him pull me to him. He settled his hands on my waist and gave me the choice to keep the distance, or close it. I reached up and wrapped my arms around his neck, allowing him to put his hands at the small of my back, just above my ass. His palms burned through the thin fabric of my dress and desire hit me strong enough to make my knees weak.

We didn't talk as we moved to the music, letting our bodies find their natural rhythm, find the rhythm that the two of us had together. A lot of people, myself included, thought that dancing was a good indicator of how two people would be when they had sex. If the past couple minutes told me anything, it was that this man would rock my world.

"Would you like to go somewhere more private?" His fingers flexed on my back, the strength in them making my stomach lurch.

I hadn't come here for this. I hadn't intended to come to a club to find someone to fuck. I'd wanted to scope it out, maybe see what it was about this place that appealed to Jace. Maybe see him. Observe him. It hadn't been about sex.

But the man holding me, waiting for me to answer his question, *he* was clearly about sex. Walking, talking sex. And I wanted it.

Plus, there was always the chance that some hot and heavy fucking would help me keep my head on straight about the sexy artist in the coming weeks.

I nodded, then threaded my fingers between this stranger's and let him lead me toward the back of the club. I assumed we were on our way to a back exit, then to a hotel or his place, but instead, he stopped in front of a discreet door for a moment, doing something I couldn't see, and then it swung open.

"Well, shit." I couldn't stop the curse as I followed him into the room, but his soft laugh told me he didn't mind.

The lighting was only a little brighter in here than it was in the main room, but it was enough for me to see that the walls held whips and crops and floggers, as well as other things I had no name for. A bed sat against one wall, posters on each corner. I could see restraints on the closer two, so I assumed a matching set were on the far ones. There was also a tall chest of drawers, and a few other pieces of furniture I didn't recognize, but could guess at their uses.

"This is your first time here," he said as a statement instead of a question.

"It shows, huh?" I glanced over at him.

One side of his mouth tipped upward in a crooked smile. "I won't be offended if you back out."

I turned toward him, wrapped my arms around his neck, and pressed my body against his as I stretched up to brush my lips across his. "The hell I will."

He was still laughing when he covered my mouth with his. I felt the kiss all the way down to my toes, in every cell of my body. His tongue stroked mine, but before we could deepen the connection, our masks bumped together.

His fingers threaded through my hair. "Should we take off our masks?"

My stomach flipped. I didn't know who he was, and while I was desperate to discover what was under those clothes, I wasn't sure I was ready to share our identities.

"Would it change things if I said no?"

He smiled at me. "Not at all. I have no problem with a little mystery." He gave me a soft kiss, then stepped back.

"But since I won't be able to see much in the way of facial expressions, we need to have a safe word in place."

I knew what that was, at least. "Do you have a suggestion?"

"I usually prefer *yellow* and *red,* so we have a *slowdown* and a *stop*."

That answered any question I had about whether or not he'd done this before. Strangely enough, it didn't bother me. If anything, it made me confident that the two of us could have something in the here and now, and then go our separate ways without any hard feelings or expectations.

"Works for me."

I started to reach behind me to unzip my dress, but he stopped me with a hand on my arm.

"In here, I'm in charge." He didn't shout, and it wasn't some macho declaration either. It was a simple, profound statement. Then he waited to see what I'd do.

"All right." I dropped my hand and tried not to show how much his words affected me. I shouldn't have found it so hot, shouldn't have craved what he offered. But I did. "Be in charge."

His eyes narrowed, like he was trying to figure me out, and I felt a stab of fear. I didn't want that, didn't want this to be something complicated. I was taking a giant step out of my comfort zone, moving toward something new and probably crazy. I didn't need to also worry about someone trying to get inside my head.

I didn't know how much of what I was feeling reflected on the small section of my face he could see, but he must have seen something because he took a step back and began unbuttoning his shirt.

He didn't have to tell me to watch, because I couldn't take my eyes off him. Fuck, he was gorgeous. Tanned skin and firm, defined muscles, a trail of golden curls starting at his belly button and going down until they disappeared beneath the waistband of his pants. And those tattoos...swirls of black in elegant Celtic designs. I wanted to trace each and every one of them with my tongue.

He folded his shirt carefully and draped it over a nearby chair. Without a word, he walked around behind me, and a moment later, I felt his hands on my zipper. As he slowly lowered it, he pressed his lips to my ear. "I knew you'd never done this before from the moment I saw you walk in tonight. Most submissives don't look a Dom in the eyes. They keep their heads down. But you didn't. I knew you weren't a Dom either."

I wasn't sure if I was allowed to ask a question, but I did it anyway. "How?"

I sucked in a breath as his fingertips grazed my back. That small touch shouldn't feel that good. Everything about this was impossible. Taking control by giving it up. Revealing intimate parts of my body while hiding my face.

A desire so strong that I was no longer sure that I had the power over my own body to stop myself.

He kissed my neck even as he pushed my dress off my shoulders. "Because you want to submit to me."

I closed my eyes. Fuck. How in the world could this stranger have known that about me when I hadn't even figured it out about myself?

"For tonight, while we're in this room, let go. You're safe with me. You say the safe words, and I'll stop, but until then, trust me to know what you need."

His hands slid around me and cupped my breasts. I let out a soft moan that turned into a cry when he rolled my nipples between his finger and thumb. The touch was rougher than I expected, but it didn't make me want to run. It made me arch my back, push my breasts against his talented hands.

"Bend over the end of the bed, palms flat on the mattress. I'm going to make you scream."

What the *fuck* had I gotten myself into?

NINE
JACE

I hadn't felt this good in a long time. I went to the club last night after Erik called to ask me to keep an eye on Alix. There'd still been no word from Alix's girl, and he wasn't getting any better. He hadn't showed, and I was pissed considering I'd been wearing a fucking mask...but then I'd seen *her*.

After I left Gilded Cage last night, I kept waiting for the good feeling to fade. Sure, the encounter had been the best sex I'd had since I couldn't remember when, but it was more than just sex. I couldn't deny that. I'd never understood the appeal of having a complete novice, but the moment I saw my mystery woman across the room, I hadn't cared about her experience or anything other than having her.

I didn't use my hands. Ever. I used floggers and whips

and crops and even belts, but I never used my bare hands to spank a one-session hook up. Somehow, it seemed too personal. It had never been an issue before, because I'd never wanted to do it. Until last night...

The moment I brought my hand down on that perfect ass I knew that I wasn't going to be using anything but my hands on this woman. I had to feel every inch of her, had to know the silken whisper of her skin against my palms. She gasped as I slapped her ass hard enough to sting, but she didn't ask me to stop, just like she hadn't protested when I pinched her nipples until she groaned. That had been my test to determine if she would be open to what I wanted. I planned on testing her limits, but I'd never make a woman do something she truly didn't want to do.

The music from the club played in the background, but I focused on the sound of my hand against the firm muscles of her ass, her harsh breaths, and little gasps of pleasure. My cock pressed painfully against my zipper, and I knew I wouldn't be able to take as much time as I wanted tonight. I excelled at self-control, but this was one battle I knew I would lose.

I wasn't so sure I could actually consider anything that happened last night a loss, but I definitely hadn't been as much in control as I would have liked. But after her skin turned hot and pink under my hands, after I touched every inch of her, I hadn't been able to draw things out. She'd been writhing under me, making these insanely hot noises, and I hadn't been able to wait. It hadn't mattered that I wanted to taste her, to make her come with my mouth and tongue, to make her beg for it. I barely remembered to put on the condom, and then I'd been buried inside her.

I'd come so hard that my vision had gone white.

Afterwards, we hadn't talked, but the silence between us hadn't been awkward. She handed me my shirt, and I zipped up her dress. We smiled and walked back into the club, then had gone our separate ways. No names. No exchange of phone numbers or promises to meet again.

Hell, I didn't even know what she looked like beyond being a brunette.

But I knew what she felt like.

And now I was back in the studio, itching to create, wondering if I could somehow make my mystery woman come alive. The thing was, I didn't think I could do it with paints or charcoal. I was a talented artist, though the human form wasn't usually my subject, but I didn't think I had the skill to do her justice.

At least not on canvas.

There was another option though. One that I hadn't used in more than twenty years. Not since...

I shook my head and forced that memory back. I didn't want any shadows around today. Not when I was feeling so good. Not when I was walking over to the closet where I kept my supplies, hoping that the unopened package would still be there.

I hadn't used any form of clay since I was a child, but about six months after I moved in here, my father told me that I was able to buy whatever I wanted. Any other child who'd been given such carte blanche – and the money to pull it off – might have gone nuts with electronics and games. I'd bought paints and canvases and pencils and everything I needed to draw and paint to my heart's content.

And I'd picked up a small box of clay.

I'd thrown in away a year or so later, but the pattern had repeated itself every couple years, as if a part of me couldn't quite bear to give it up completely. As I carried the box back to the table, I was glad I'd gotten it, because I had a feeling it was the only medium that might be able to capture the picture in my head.

I sat down, took a deep breath, and opened the box.

"MR. RANDALL." My housekeeper stuck her head into the studio. "Sorry to bother you."

I stared at her for nearly a full half minute before I realized I hadn't even heard her come in. I glanced toward the clock and saw that I'd been working all morning. I hadn't lost time like that in years.

"Yes?"

"There's a woman here to see you." She didn't look

happy about delivering that particular message. "She's in the kitchen and refuses to leave until–"

"Jace, sweetheart, I tried explaining to the help that you'd be thrilled to see me."

Everything in me turned to ice as the owner of the unfortunately familiar voice stepped around my housekeeper and pushed her way into my studio.

Shit.

Bianca Evison. All curves and milk chocolate skin, both of which she loved to show off. Judging by the tight, low-cut, daffodil-yellow dress she was wearing, that hadn't changed since she dumped me four years ago.

"What are you doing here?" The question came out a little more bluntly than I intended, but I was still too stunned to manage the mask I'd always needed with her.

"I came to see you, of course." She gave me the same seductive smile that had drawn me to her seven years ago at the Gilded Cage. "It's been too long, Jay."

I didn't bother correcting her. In the time we were together, I'd told her more than once that I didn't like the nickname Jay. She hadn't listened during the three years we'd been together, so why would this be any different?

I stood but didn't move any closer to her. "It's been four years, Bianca."

Her gaze dropped to my clay-covered hands and her nose wrinkled in disgust. Suddenly more self-conscious than I'd been in years, I rubbed my hands on my pants, then stopped as I realized what I was doing. This was my home. My studio. If she didn't like it, she could get the hell out.

"Seriously, why are you here?"

She came even closer, moved as if she meant to lean on the table, then thought better of it. She'd cut her raven-black hair even shorter than it was before, but those dark eyes were the same. Teasing while lust hid something sharper.

"I just moved back to the city and thought I'd look up some old friends." She looked around, then delivered one of those back-handed comments I'd ignored for far too long. "I knew you'd still be here, by yourself, and thought you'd be as happy to see me as I am to see you."

I turned my back on her and walked across the room to the sink. I knew the question she wanted me to ask, and if it would get her out of here faster, I'd play the game. "Where were you?"

"You haven't heard?" She almost sounded offended. "I married a French diplomat. I've been all over this country and France."

I had heard. In fact, I heard he claimed to be some sort of French aristocrat who'd been made a diplomat on the request of his father...but that he'd neglected to mention that said father had been arrested in some sort of scandal involving a barely legal babysitter and her mom. Bianca had dated me because I was rich, but when I hadn't proposed after three years, she'd traded up for someone who could give her the money and prestige she felt she deserved. And when that hadn't panned out, she'd filed for divorce.

Irreconcilable differences, of course.

"It didn't work out though," she said, a note of sadness so real in her voice that I would have believed it...if I hadn't known her intimately enough to know all of her tells and lies.

"Sorry to hear that," I said flatly. "If you don't mind, I'm working."

She shot another disgusted look around the room. "Oh, yes, I can see that."

I turned to see her poke one finely manicured nail into the hand I'd been sculpting, and my temper snapped. "What the *hell*, Bianca? Why would you do that?"

Her eyes widened, then narrowed. "It's just some...actually, I don't know what the fuck it is, but it shouldn't be more important than seeing your girlfriend after so long."

"Ex," I growled. "And I don't have time for this. I have a show coming up, and an art critic who's doing a piece on me. I have work to do."

I walked over to the door and opened it, then looked back at her. "You saw yourself in, so see yourself out."

TEN
SAVANNAH

My skin was on fire. Fuck that. My whole body *was on fire. Not just my ass where my exceptionally hot mystery man had been teaching me about something else he apparently knew I wanted. Who knew that being spanked was as erotic in real life as it was in fiction?*

But that wasn't the only thing he'd been doing with those strong hands of his. After he finished spanking me, he slid his hands over my hips, thumbs brushing against the edges of my overly sensitive skin. I could feel the urgency in his touch, but he didn't give in, not yet. He traced my ribs, cupped my breasts. As one hand started to play with my nipples, rolling and tugging them in turn, he moved his free hand down between my legs.

When he first told me that he'd make me scream, I

thought he'd just been bragging the same way men always bragged about their sexual prowess.

But then his fingers slipped between my folds, and he cursed. That was when I knew he'd make good on his promise.

He stroked his thumb over my clit, pleasure building with an intensity and speed I hadn't known before. Then his fingers were inside me. Strong, calloused fingers that twisted and rubbed all the good places.

I gave a cry of pleasure when I came, and then he was pulling me up onto the bed, the bedspread rubbing against my throbbing nipples. He moved between my legs, the thick head of his cock nudging against my entrance. His fingers dug into my hips as he held me firm, then drove into me in one smooth stroke.

I felt his control shatter as he pounded into me, and I pressed my face against the thick bedspread, screaming just like he promised...

I came awake with a start, heart racing, breath coming in pants, my body hanging on the edge of a climax. The same thing happened last night as well, and even though my ass wasn't as sore today as it had been yesterday, it was still tender enough to remind me that I hadn't imagined any of it. It had been more memory than dream, but it still hadn't done that night justice.

All the same, I closed my eyes again and slid my hand under my sheets. I learned last night that I wouldn't get any rest if I didn't take care of things myself. Fortunately, between how tightly wound my dream had made me, and how skilled I'd become at finding my own release, it took only a few well-placed touches for me to come.

It would take more than a couple climaxes, however, before Tuesday night got out of my head. And even longer until I forgot the masked man who'd made me realize that his world might be one I'd like to spend a little more time in.

Or maybe a lot.

I STARED up at the house for a moment, still in awe as much as I had been the first time. At least that was what I told myself. Because it couldn't be that I was interested in seeing Jace again. Not after the way the masked man had made my body sing. I found Jace...interesting. From a professional standpoint. That was all.

Even so, it was the late morning heat more than anything that had me walking over to the side door and knocking.

"Is Mr. Randall expecting you?"

I turned to see a middle-aged woman standing at the corner of the house. She possessed the stern sort of look that told me she'd know if I lied.

"Not exactly," I admitted. "I was here earlier this week

and mentioned that I'd be coming back. I tried calling ahead, but he didn't answer."

"And you are...?"

"Savannah Birch." I smiled, but made sure it wasn't too wide. I didn't want her to think I was trying to charm her. "I'm an art critic who's doing a piece on Mr. Randall's new show."

She came toward me, a skeptical expression on her face. "You don't look old enough to be an art critic."

"Thank you."

That finally got a partial smile out of her. "You're not going to do anything to hurt Mr. Randall, are you?"

What a strange question. I shook my head. "Not at all."

No matter how confusing the connection between the two of us, there was nothing negative about it. Besides, I couldn't imagine anyone hurting someone as amazing as Jace.

"All right then," she said, giving me a hard look. "I believe you."

She reached past me, tapped in a few numbers to the keypad by the door, and then opened it. "He's been in the studio almost non-stop since yesterday morning. See if you can get him to stop for some food. He forgets to eat when he gets like this."

I thanked her and headed inside. I'd worn soft-soled flats today, so I didn't make any noise as I moved into the studio. His back was to me, giving me the opportunity to watch him work how he did when no one else was around.

Which apparently meant wearing only a pair of worn jeans. No shoes. No shirt.

Damn.

I knew he had a nice build, but even my imagination hadn't pictured just how broad his shoulders were, how defined the muscles of his back.

I could see his arms moving, but not what he was doing. It didn't quite look like he was painting; the movements were too close for that. Curiosity overcame my desire to continue being able to watch from the shadows.

"Jace?" I took a few steps toward him.

As he turned, I saw that he wasn't painting. His hands were smeared with what I realized was reddish-brown clay. I couldn't see what he was making, but it wasn't a picture.

But that faded into the background of my thoughts as I took in his six – no, that was an eight-pack. His muscled forearms. Toned chest covered with intricate tattoos that my fingers itched to trace...

Wait.

I knew those tattoos.

Knew them intimately.

My knees almost buckled as it hit me. Jace Randall was my masked lover.

Oh shit.

ELEVEN
JACE

For the second time in two days, I'd been so wrapped up in what I was doing that I hadn't heard someone come in until a woman spoke. Except, this time, it wasn't my housekeeper, or my ex. For a moment, as I was turning, I thought my mystery woman had found me, but then I remembered that she didn't know my identity.

Still, I was surprisingly pleased to see that it was Savannah.

"Hey." I smiled, then felt the expression falter as I realized something was off.

She looked...flustered. Considering she hadn't been flustered during our first meeting/misunderstanding, something really had to have thrown her. I took a step toward her, then finally caught on. She was staring at me...because I wasn't wearing a shirt.

Well, that was damn unprofessional of me.

"Sorry." I grinned as I looked around for my shirt. "I didn't know you were coming."

She licked her lips and managed a smile, but the expression looked forced as hell. "Yeah, I called, but you must not have gotten my message." The smile grew wider, but something about her expression was still a little tight. Of course, that could've been me projecting.

I frowned and grabbed my shirt from where it had fallen off the table, possibly because I'd thrown it without really looking. My phone, however, had been carefully set on the table...and then completely forgotten.

"I was in the zone." I picked it up and saw that she'd called twice and left a voicemail. I also saw a rambling text from Alix that he'd clearly sent when he was drunk, which meant he wasn't expecting a reply. "Did you forget to ask me something the other day?"

"No," she said quickly, licking her lips again. My cock pulsed, and I stuffed my arms into my shirt as a distraction from how she affected me. "I mean, sort of. I wanted to talk to you about your process. For the article. But if you're busy..." She looked toward the door.

"Not at all," I said before I could think better of it. "I should probably take a break for lunch anyway."

"Is that something new?" She gestured behind me.

I reached up to scratch the back of my head, then remembered I had clay on my hands. I went to the sink and started to wash up. "Yeah, it's something I just started the other day."

"Is it for the show?"

Her voice sounded strange, and as I looked over, I saw her staring down at my half-completed sculpture. I felt heat flood my cheeks. I hadn't really been thinking about the show when I started working. I'd simply been focused on getting my vision out.

"I haven't decided," I answered honestly.

"I've never seen you work with clay before," she said without looking at me. She seemed almost mesmerized by it as she walked around the table for different angles. "What made you decide to change things with such a short amount of time before your show?"

I opened my mouth to give her some sort of random, vague answer. I could say that my inspiration couldn't be conveyed through painting, because that was true...but it wasn't really the truth.

Maybe it was time to tell it.

"How about we talk about it over coffee?"

TWELVE
SAVANNAH

I knew he'd asked me to coffee as one professional to another, a way for him to get something to eat while he put up with my questions. I knew he only saw me as the reporter he'd talked to a couple days ago. And I knew the moment he said my name that he didn't have a clue that we'd had slightly kinky sex at a BDSM club the other night.

But that didn't stop me from hoping that he might want something more from me. Like maybe another couple hours of insanely hot fucking.

I considered myself a confident woman, but I hadn't been arrogant enough to think that one night with me had inspired an artist like Jace. Until I saw what he'd been sculpting.

Me.

Or, more specifically, what he would have seen of me while I was bent over the bed as he spanked the hell out of me.

My hips, back, and ass. I hadn't exactly spent much time looking at myself from that angle, but there was only so much I could credit to coincidence.

Now I needed to figure out what I was going to do about it. He didn't know my face, and I didn't have any identifying tattoos, so he could include that sculpture in his show and no one would be the wiser. But could I consider myself an unbiased critic if I'd slept with the artist? If he used me as a model, however unknowingly?

And what did it mean that he sculpted me.

"Chestnut Praline Latte," Jace said as he set my order down in front of me. "And a turkey on rye."

I lifted the cup to my nose and inhaled. "Thanks."

He waited until we'd both taken the edge off our hunger to start talking. "When I was six, my mom and I didn't have any money for Christmas presents, so we went to this mission. Someone – I never could find out who – had donated this amazing art kit, and I started experimenting with everything in it. Paints. Charcoals. All kinds of things. It became how I expressed myself, how I dealt with the world around me."

There wasn't much out there about Jace's life before he came to live with his father at the age of ten. Enough had gotten out about his mother that it was generally assumed that she'd been a stripper, possibly even a prostitute, but Benjamin Gooding had been well-liked and well-connected, so most people didn't bother trying to dig too deep. Now, I wondered if Jace's father had worked to keep things quiet for his son's sake.

He shifted in his seat, some of the ease leaving him. "The thing I loved the most was this little container of sculpting clay. I made all sorts of little things for my mom, for our apartment. One day, I made a special one for her birthday, and when I surprised her with it, the guy she was seeing got upset and smashed it. Every single thing I made was destroyed and thrown away."

My gut told me there was more to the story than he was telling, and the shadow in his eyes said it wasn't good. My heart ached for the little boy he'd been, and I knew I couldn't ask him for any more than that. Not without hurting him more, and I wouldn't have done it even before we slept together.

"That's awful." I reached across the table and put my hand over his. To my surprise, he didn't pull away.

"Thanks." The smile he gave me held a little less darkness in its depths.

The moment gave me the courage I needed to ask one of the questions bouncing around in my head. "Can I ask who the model is?"

His eyebrows shot up. "The model?"

"For the sculpture." I pulled my hand back and tried to

pass it off as me wanting a drink. I could feel the flush creeping up my cheeks as I tried to sound nonchalant. "None of your other work had people in it, so I was wondering who not only got you to break away from your usual subject, but brought you back to your favorite medium."

He rubbed his hand on the back of his neck, then up over his head, making a mess of his hair. To my surprise, his ears were turning red. "I met someone who...inspired me."

I tried not to let the hope flickering inside me grow. I didn't want to read too much into his statement. Inspiration didn't mean that he wanted another night with me, especially if he found out my identity.

But it didn't mean I'd be able to just let it go either.

Dammit. I needed to talk to someone about this, which meant I was going to have to confess to someone about everything.

Dammit.

Everett was never going to let me live it down.

WHEN I WAS a student at NYU, I hadn't spent much time in the physics department unless I was looking for Everett, so nothing much had changed except for the fact that instead of coming from the Art and English departments, I came from home or work.

Everett had classes today and wasn't working tonight, so I went to the building that held his last class of the day and waited in the hallway. As I leaned against the wall, I tried to run through the outline I held in my head for my article, but every time I came to some conclusion, something else about Jace would draw my attention. I'd either find myself thinking about the heat I'd seen in his eyes at the club, or the way it had felt to dance with him, or how easy it was to talk to him.

"You're late," I snapped as Everett came out of the classroom. "Everyone else left five minutes ago."

Everett raised an eyebrow. "Damn. Someone either needs to get laid or deal with whatever PMS issues you have going on right now."

I sighed. "Shit. I'm sorry." I pushed my hair back from my face. "How about I buy dinner and tell you what's got me biting your head off?"

He scrubbed his palms together. "I get to choose the place."

I glared at him. "Seriously? You're going to negotiate an apologetic gesture?"

He gave me that easy grin that I loved. "Of course."

I rolled my eyes and let myself fall into the ease of being with my best friend. I could have called Lei or Lorde and talked to them, but even as much as I loved them, Everett was the only one I could completely confide in about this. I didn't blurt it out while we were walking though. No, this called for dinner...and alcohol.

Lots of alcohol.

By the time we were both buzzed enough to have the conversation, the diner Everett had chosen was full and noisy, which was good because that meant the chances of anyone overhearing what I was about to say were slim.

"Remember me telling you that I was going to see Jace Randall on Monday?"

"Yes," he said, leaning forward. He knew we were about to get to the good stuff. "I also remember you promising to call me and dish on all the dirty details, but that hadn't happened."

"You're really enjoying guilt tripping me here, aren't you?" I threw a french fry at him.

"I am." He popped the fry into his mouth.

"Well, I've got some great dirty details for you," I said wryly. "You just have to promise that this stays between us because it's a bit...well, you'll understand when I tell you."

"Now I'm intrigued." He leaned toward me ever farther. "My lips are sealed. Spill."

So, spill I did.

I told him about meeting Jace for the first time, and that I'd been attracted but had tried to stay professional. Then I told him about going to the club and watched his eyes grow wider until he finally let out a low whistle.

"So, you're torn between the artist who made you love art, and a mystery man who rocked your world?"

I'd paused to drain the last of my beer, and now I shook my head. "I'm in trouble because my mystery man *is* the artist."

"No fucking way." Everett's voice was low, his eyes nearly bulging out of his head. "I thought you said you didn't exchange names and you didn't see his face."

"I didn't." I rubbed my temples as my head throbbed. "But I did see the tattoos on his chest and upper arms. Then today, when I went to see Jace to talk about the article, he had his shirt off, and–"

"And you saw the tattoos." Everett whistled again. "Does he know? That you and he–"

"No." I shook my head. "And that's not all. He was making a sculpture when I got there, and it was...*me*."

"Shit." Everett stared at me. "You really stepped in it, Sav. What are you going to do?"

"I don't know," I admitted. "Why the hell do you think I'm talking to you about it?"

THIRTEEN
SAVANNAH

Why had I listened to Everett?

I asked myself the same question for the tenth time since I got home last night. It sounded like a great idea when we were at the diner talking about it, but when I was alone, I started questioning the wisdom of it, and I'd just gotten more uncertain throughout the day today.

But I was still walking toward the front door of the club, the mask I'd forgotten to return clutched in my hand. Part of me was hoping I'd run into Jace before I had the chance to put the mask on, and I wouldn't have to make any decisions about what to do when I saw him.

Because that was the one thing that neither Everett nor I had been able to agree on, partially because I couldn't decide if I wanted to come clean or not. I could leave things as they were between Jace and myself, keep our one night together as a special memory, and continue with my piece on Jace as if nothing had happened. That would be the smartest thing to do, both professionally and personally.

And yet here I was, wearing a sexy red dress that I found buried at the back of my closet, ready to put myself out there on the off chance that this thing I'd felt between us hadn't been a fluke.

I smoothed my hands over my dress, but it didn't really need it considering it fit like it'd been painted on. It had been an impulsive purchase during a shopping spree with Lei and Lorde during our last spring break, and I'd only worn it once. I was confident in my sexuality, but this was the sort of thing designed to attract attention, and I'd never really wanted that before tonight.

I was a bit worried that the man at the door would confiscate the mask, and maybe even kick me out since I'd accidentally absconded with it, but he didn't do anything other than nod at me as I walked past. As soon as I was inside, I saw that the masquerade night must have been for the whole week because everyone else was still wearing masks. I quickly put mine on and moved off to the side to watch and wait.

I'd been there only a few minutes when I sensed someone come up beside me. Before I could turn and look, I caught the unmistakable scent of spice and clay and man. Jace.

"I hoped I'd see you here tonight."

"Likewise." My voice was surprisingly steady despite my nerves.

"Come with me."

He took my hand, his grip on my fingers loose enough that I could pull free if I wanted to. Instead of doing that, I let him pull me after him. As we made our way toward the back of the club, I tried to think of what I'd say to him when we were alone, but even as he closed the door behind us a few moments later, my mind was blank.

"You look incredibly beautiful," he said as he slid his hands up my arms.

Now that I knew who he was, I could tell he was using his hands to learn my body, just like he had before.

"Thank you," I said. "You do too."

He wore a fitted charcoal gray short-sleeved shirt and a pair of jeans that hugged his firm thighs and ass. He had on the same mask as the other night, but even though his outfit was more casual, he managed to pull off this one as well as the other.

"So..." I took a deep breath to gather my courage. "I was wondering if, this time, we could take off the masks. See each other."

He went so still that I wondered for a moment if I'd said the wrong thing. Then he offered me a smile that seemed a bit tight. "How about this? We leave them on while we see if we really do have chemistry together, and if we still want to reveal our identities after, we can do it then."

I wanted to get this out of the way, to know for certain that Jace wanted *me* and not just masked mystery me. But I wanted to be with him one more time even more. Especially since I didn't know if I'd get the chance once he learned who I was.

I nodded. "All right. We'll do this your way."

His smile widened into the wicked sort of grin that tied my stomach in knots. "I thought we agreed last time that when we're in here, *everything* is my way."

Fuck.

All I could do was stand there as he lowered his head. His eyes blazed as his mouth came down on mine. The edge of my mask pressed into my face, but I didn't mind. If this was going to be the last time he kissed me, the last time I would know what it was like to be claimed by him, then I almost wished for something that would leave a lasting impression.

His tongue plundered my mouth, and his hands dug into my hips, pulling me so tightly against him that I could feel the ridge of his cock pressing against my stomach through his zipper. I pushed up on my toes, desperate to feel that pressure and friction against the place I needed it the most. He groaned as I nipped his bottom lip, then soothed the sting with my tongue.

"I couldn't stop thinking about you," he confessed as he

broke the kiss. He rested his forehead against mine, his grip tightening as if he was afraid I'd walk away.

Not that there was a chance in hell of that happening. I was in too fucking deep.

"What were you thinking?" I whispered the question because I didn't trust my voice not to shake. Knowing that he'd been thinking about me, maybe even when he'd been opening up to me about his past, gave me hope, however tenuous, that he might not be disappointed when he saw who I was.

His fingers flexed, as if he wasn't quite as tightly contained as he seemed. "So many things."

I shivered at the dark promise in those words. I might have been a bit nervous at all the possibilities, but fear was definitely not one of the emotions I was feeling at the moment. Knowing that he was Jace made me trust him more, not less.

"Tell me." I supposed it could have seemed like a demand – which even I knew was a no-no for someone in a submissive position – but it sounded more like a plea. Which, I guessed, in a way it was. If this was going to be our final time together, I wanted to know as much about him as possible.

"You're new to this," he said, "I don't want to frighten you."

I closed my eyes as another shiver went through me, this one of anticipation. "I want to know. Please." His name was on the tip of my tongue and it took everything I had not to call him by it. "What have you been thinking about me?"

"How much I want to push you," he finally confessed. "How I want to learn your limits, and then take you places that you've never thought possible. I want to test your pain threshold by showing you just how good it can be to hurt, how pain can make pleasure so much more exquisite, more intense."

I silently swore. I told myself that I would be okay if this was it, if we ended here, but listening to him talk, my nipples were already hard, my pussy throbbing and wet. How could I give this up? How could I walk away and never feel this way again?

Still, I couldn't even begin to imagine what it would be like if we went past tonight. How could a person survive something like what he described? Survive that kind of intensity? I'd burst into flames if I was subjected to this daily.

But what a way to go.

"I thought about all the ways I could make you scream again," he continued, his voice rough. "How beautiful your skin would look with red stripes from a flogger. The sounds you would make when I put clamps on your nipples. And then the even hotter ones when I removed them. The way you would curse and writhe, tugging on restraints while I took you to the edge over and over again, but never quite let you get there."

I'd spent too much time trying to argue with myself about the things I secretly wanted for years. I wasn't a virgin, and I wasn't a prude, but I'd always kept this part of myself under tight wraps. Now, he set it out there in a way I knew was meant to run me off. Instead, it drew me to him, knowing that the things he wanted to do to me fit with what I wanted done. Unlike previous lovers, he wouldn't balk at the experiences I wanted to try. If anything, he would want more.

If he decided he was willing to try for more than just tonight.

"Choose," I said quietly. "Choose what you want for tonight."

He stiffened, then pulled back enough so that his eyes could meet mine. For one heart-stopping second, I thought he recognized me, then he spoke, and I knew my identity was still a secret.

"I'll only ask this once, and after that, you'll have to use the safe words to stop me." His thumbs made circles on my hips, as if he was already imagining his answer to my quasi-demand. "Are you sure you want this?"

I didn't even hesitate. "Yes." Then, unable to stop with a simple one-word answer, I added, "How do you want me?"

FOURTEEN
JACE

How in the *hell* was I supposed to answer *that* question?

A stranger shouldn't be able to get under my skin like this. Then again, I wasn't supposed to want a novice this badly. I shouldn't have spent so many hours thinking of all the things I wanted to introduce her to...or thinking of how I wanted to dismember any other man who would dare to take my place when I stepped aside. Because I had no doubt there would be many of them lining up to train her to be their perfect sub.

Just like I had no doubt that I was rapidly becoming addicted to this woman and that was a dangerous thing.

But it wasn't enough to stop me from lowering my head to kiss her again, to taste her.

I began to strip away her clothes as my tongue slid across hers. I needed to have my hands on her impossibly soft skin, feel her shudder under my touch. And I wanted to see all of her, savor every moment.

I still didn't know what I was going to do afterwards, if I would remove my mask and reveal my identity, but I knew I wanted tonight to leave an impression that made all past and future lovers insignificant. That would make it so that she would never, could never, forget me.

She moaned as I lowered her to the bed, my thigh pressing against the wet silk between her legs. Damn. I'd known women who'd gotten turned on easily, but nothing like this.

"I'm going to tie you up," I informed her as I reluctantly straightened. Part of me wanted nothing more than to bury myself inside her right now, but I knew waiting would make it all the sweeter. "And then, I'm going to see how many times I can get you close to the edge before you beg me to let you come."

Her breathing hitched, her small, perfect breasts straining against the sheer, pale lace of her bra. I could see the dusky peach color of her nipples and my mouth watered. I would wait though, to find out what it was like to taste her. I'd taken her too fast before, hadn't taken the time to savor her.

I intended to remedy that mistake.

The moment she nodded, I picked her up and carried her over to the bed. We could have just walked, but I needed my hands on her. Before I lowered her on to the mattress, I bent my head to brush my lips across hers. It was the most chaste of our kisses, but it still sent an electric tingle through me.

Damn.

I was glad I'd decided to tie her up, because I needed a few minutes to regain my self-control. That, I thought, was part of the draw. I loved being in charge, but recently, much of the thrill had waned. It wasn't until I met her that I realized part of the problem was that most of the challenge was gone. I still enjoyed the BDSM side of things, and the sex itself, but nothing much beyond the physical. The women I fucked were beautiful in a variety of ways, but there was no seduction, nothing...special.

This woman though. Something about her drew me, made me want her like I hadn't wanted anything in a long time. One time hadn't been enough, and as I finished fastening the last restraint, I wondered if this time would satisfy that need inside me.

I wasn't going to think about that now. Not when I had a beautiful, half-clothed woman tied up and waiting for me to make good on my promise to show her just how close to the edge I could push her.

Her eyes were wide as I looked down at her, but there was no sign of fear in those pale depths, only trust and desire. I ran my fingers up her calf and over her knees as I knelt between her spread legs. As I reached her thighs and hips, I spread my hands out so that my whole hand moved across her ribs, and then up to cup her breasts, before moving back down again.

"Yes," she breathed as I stroked her soft skin, as my thumbs and fingers found her pebbled nipples.

As I teased her sensitive flesh, I watched her face and found that I wished I could see more of her, that I could see every bit of her expression as I brought her pleasure, that I would know *exactly* what she looked like when she came.

I hooked my fingers in the cups of her bra and pulled them down. Fuck. She had the most gorgeous breasts. I couldn't resist lowering my head and flicking my tongue across the tips of her nipples. She swore, a shiver running through her, and then swore again as I circled the darker flesh with the tip of my tongue.

I pulled my shirt over my head and tossed it to the side, then stripped off my pants. My erection was tenting out the front of my boxer briefs, and when her tongue darted out to run along her slightly swollen lips, I almost came right then.

For a moment, I wasn't sure whose control was being tested.

Then I had my mouth on the underside of her breast, sucking hard enough to leave a mark before moving up to her nipple. She began to gasp and twist as best she could, but the only sounds were ones of pure pleasure, so I kept going, working teeth and tongue and lips until I could feel her pulling on her restraints.

I raised my head and seriously considered ripping off both of our masks right then and there. My lovely sub was so close, I could see it in her eyes. I locked her gaze with mine, then pressed my knee between her legs. Her panties were soaked as I leaned into her, letting my leg put the right amount of pressure against the places she needed it the most.

"Fuck." Her eyes rolled back even as her hips began to move against me.

I let her have a couple moments working herself against my knee, and I enjoyed watching every one of them before I backed off. She made a sound of protest that almost had me giving in, but I knew it'd be worth it to follow through.

"I've got you, gorgeous," I said as I stretched out between her legs. "But it's not time to come yet."

"Please," she begged.

I turned my head and pressed my lips high on her inner thigh, sucking the sweet smelling skin into my mouth. After I marked her, I turned my attention to the place I'd been dreaming about from the first moment I saw her. After teasing her through the thin fabric of her panties for a few seconds, I pulled on them until they gave with a loud tearing sound. Then I buried my face between her legs and drove her to the edge.

Again.

And again.

And again.

Until I was the one who couldn't take it anymore, and I let her tip over into a screaming orgasm that made me grateful the room was soundproofed.

Then I was inside her again and it was like everything good I'd ever known in my life rolled together into this time, this place, with this person.

And I wasn't sure I could let her go.

I SHOULD HAVE BEEN RELAXED, sated, after what we'd just done, but as I watched her dress, my stomach began to twist. Not because of what we'd done, but because this was it, the moment where I had to decide what I wanted. The two of us could go our separate ways, maybe hook up again once or twice more in the future without ever knowing who the other person was. Or, we could remove our masks, exchange names, and find out if this was something we wanted to explore.

I couldn't deny that I found some liberty in the fact that she didn't know who I was, that while she might guess that I had money, it couldn't have been a true deciding factor in her choosing me that first night. But as soon as I said I wanted us to take off our masks, everything would change.

And none of that was enough to keep me from wanting to see her face, from knowing who she was. I didn't know if the connection between us would last without the mystery, but I wanted to try.

"If you're still interested, I'd like to know who you are." The words sounded casual enough, but I wasn't sure she bought it. My own heart was pounding so hard in my chest that I was certain she'd be able to hear it.

I'd never thought of myself as a shallow person, and my biggest fear at this moment was that seeing her would prove me wrong. I'd never be able to live with myself if she showed me who she was and my attraction to her disappeared when I saw her face. Personality conflicts and that sort of thing would be understandable, but if I didn't find her attractive and I didn't want to be with her because of that, I'd hate myself.

She straightened, hands trembling as she smoothed down her dress. That gesture alone was enough to heighten my anxiety, but I reminded myself that she didn't know who I was, so she was probably just as nervous as I was about the whole situation. Her gaze flicked to my face and then away again.

"I'd like that." Her voice was soft, but no less determined. "Are you sure?"

I almost frowned at the question, wondering what had

prompted it, but I was more interested in learning her identity than I was in chasing a question. I knew if I started digging at her intentions like I had everyone else in the past, I'd talk myself out of something that could end up being the best part of my life.

As an answer, I reached up and pulled off my mask. I waited for a response for a split second before realizing she was taking off her mask as well. Very slowly, it lowered, revealing large eyes...nose...lips...chin.

It was her.

I swore, vilely and loudly.

How in the *hell* had I not known I'd been fucking Savannah Birch?

In the next moment, I realized that she wasn't freaking out. If anything, the look on her face was slightly sheepish.

"You knew." I didn't make it a question because I didn't need to. It was written right there on her expression. "You knew it was me." It sounded like an accusation this time.

She nodded and licked her lips. "Not the first time. When I walked into your studio the other day and you weren't wearing a shirt." Her cheeks grew pink. "I recognized your tattoos."

My stomach churned, bile rising up in my throat. "Tonight?"

Her face grew more red. "That's why I suggested we take the masks off."

"And when I said I wanted to wait, why didn't you stop

me?" I curled my hands into fists. "You should have told me before we..." I ran my hand through my hair. "*Shit*, Savannah. This...we...damn it all."

"I wanted..."

She didn't finish the sentence even as her face turned impossibly red, but I didn't need her to say what it was she wanted. I had a pretty good idea, because I'd wanted it too. And that just pissed me off even more.

"You should have told me." My voice was harsh enough to make her eyes widen in surprise, but I didn't let that affect me. "The moment you realized who I was. And how the hell did you get in to Gilded Cage in the first place?" I shook my head and held up my hands. "Never mind, I don't want to know. It doesn't matter anyway. We fucked. That's it. And if a single word of it makes its way into your article, or any form of media for that matter, I'll take legal action."

She stared at me for a few seconds, and I waited to see if she'd try seduction or crying, since those were pretty much the only two weapons I'd ever seen a woman wield. She didn't do either.

"Fuck you." The words came out flat and cold, with a hint of disappointment in them. "No wonder you're so alone and miserable. Don't worry, Mr. Randall, your secrets are safe. I don't want anyone knowing I fucked such a bastard."

As she turned and walked away, a seed of doubt perked up its head, and I began to wonder if I'd made a mistake, if maybe she was better than the women I'd known in the past. Better than I'd ever expected any woman to be.

Not that it mattered now. Even if I was wrong, I'd still completely fucked up any chance I ever had with her.

FIFTEEN
SAVANNAH

I was still reeling as I made my way through the club. I wanted to run, to get away from this place – and Jace – as quickly as I could. Not because I thought I was going to cry, but because the combination of anger and embarrassment coursing through me made me want to hit something or someone, and I doubted giving Jace Randall a black eye would do anything positive for my career.

I considered throwing my mask onto the bar as I passed, but I didn't want to run the risk of someone I knew spotting me and asking awkward questions. No matter how much I enjoyed sex with Jace, or how much I'd learned about my own sexual desires during those two encounters, I didn't want anything to remind me of what happened. Maybe I'd explore this part of my sexuality again at some ınt in the future, but for right now, I planned to stay as far away from men as possible.

In fact, I was going to spend the weekend finishing up everything in my article except the critique of the art itself. Once that was done, I'd forget about Jace until next month when I'd see his show. Since I'd have everything else done, I wouldn't even need to talk to him that night.

And that would be for the best.

This was the first time – and would be the last – that I compromised my journalistic integrity. If I ever found myself attracted to a subject again, I'd have this moment to remind me just what a horrible idea that was.

The mask came off as soon as I'd moved a few yards from Gilded Cage, so all I got from the cab driver was an appreciative look. I stared out the window as the city went by, trying not to think about anything, especially not the fact that I wasn't wearing any underwear because Jace had literally torn them off of me. My pussy and nipples were throbbing from the attention he'd paid them, my skin still tingling from his touch. Every cell in my body was screaming for me to go back and beg him to take me again.

"No way in *hell*," I muttered. I'd pushed down my pride once to sleep with him in the hopes that maybe he'd want more than a couple anonymous encounters. I wasn't fool enough to make that mistake twice.

By the time I reached my apartment, I was exhausted. All I wanted to do was take a hot shower and go to bed.

Fortunately, Everett was still out, so I was able to settle into my bed before he got home. Sleep wasn't so easy in coming, especially after I heard Everett and Cal trying to be quiet as they went to Everett's room. The intimate hushed laughter made my heart twist painfully, and I swore to myself that I was going to focus on work from now on. No more hot, kinky sex with masked strangers.

That seemed like the sort of promise I should be able to keep.

"MOTHERFUCKING BASTARD," I muttered as I pushed back from the table and ran my hands through my hair.

"Anyone I know?" Everett asked as he strolled out of his room. The smug smile on his face told me he'd had a far better night than the one I'd just experienced.

"Just a bit of writer's block." I wasn't completely lying. I was having a hell of a time putting my thoughts into words. Well, words that would be appropriate for public consumption anyway.

"Did you finish your interviews?" he asked as he rummaged through the fridge looking for who knew what. "Maybe you need to get to know your subject better."

It was on the tip of my tongue to tell him he knew damn well that I knew my subject intimately, but I bit it back. One, it wasn't entirely true. I had sex with Jace, but I wasn't so sure that actually counted as being intimate. And two, I didn't feel like listening to him tell me this was a conflict of interest.

Fortunately, Everett continued without seeming to notice my internal conflict. "Don't you always say that only using one source of information doesn't let you portray things in a truly unbiased light? I mean, I know you're mostly writing about the art, but shouldn't you see if what he's told you matches up with other sources?"

I sighed. He had a point. If I was going to treat Jace like I would any other subject, I needed to be just as skeptical about the truth of what he'd told me. Which meant I needed to dig deeper than I'd gone before, particularly about the parts of Jace's life I thought he glossed over.

"Thanks," I said as I got up to pour myself another cup of coffee. I was going to need massive amounts of caffeine to do this right.

When I started doing some backstory on Jace before I met him, I hadn't been surprised that there wasn't much to find. He tended to keep to the shadows, never making any sort of splash that wasn't related to his work. He wasn't a controversial artist, or one that made the news for getting into trouble. He was insanely wealthy, but stayed out of the limelight there as well. No drawing attention to himself with either entitled or overly philanthropic behavior.

There'd been very little about his relationship with his

parents, but his father had been a very private person as well. After hearing Jace's story about how he'd fallen in love with art, I knew there had to be more that wasn't being said. Everything was simply too vague.

So I started to dig.

Online sources. Reaching out to contacts. Sorting fact from fiction and speculation until, by Sunday evening, I had a bit clearer picture of Jace's childhood. As far as I could tell, his mother was still alive. It wasn't her death that had prompted Jace to be sent to live with Benjamin Gooding, and it hadn't been Mr. Gooding's pursuit of custody either. From what I could tell, Gooding hadn't even known about Jace's existence for nearly a decade.

A decade filled with police reports of domestic violence between Veronica Randall and various boyfriends, never anything enough to warrant taking her son away though. Not until he was ten years-old, and she left him for an undetermined amount of time. The child services report stated that it could have been anywhere from five to seven weeks before someone noticed. Jace had been put in a group home for three weeks before his mother had returned.

I could find no record of her trying to regain custody of him. By all accounts, she simply showed up one day with Benjamin Gooding, announced that he was Jace's father, and then left again.

The thought of a mother doing that to her child made

my blood boil. It didn't matter that Gooding had taken care of Jace from that point on. I was glad that he had, but I couldn't imagine treating any child like that, let alone my own.

And despite my own anger toward Jace for how he'd behaved, I found myself wondering just how much all of that had left its mark. If perhaps the walls he'd constructed to keep himself safe as a child were the same ones he'd put up to push me away. I knew it was dangerous thinking like that, and that I'd probably end up getting hurt even more deeply than I already was, but I couldn't stop myself from thinking that maybe he just needed someone to fight for him instead of walking away.

SIXTEEN
JACE

To say that I hadn't gotten much sleep last night would have been an understatement. When I hadn't been plagued by visions of Savannah's gorgeous body, reminded of her scent and the feel of her skin against mine, I'd been thinking about the sick feeling in the pit of my stomach that had come when I recognized her, the way my heart had twisted when her expression had fallen, then hardened. My own hot words echoed in my ears, followed by her icy ones.

I'd spent the last hour staring up at the ceiling, wondering if there was any possible way I could have been wrong. I went through it all in my head again.

She'd never been to Gilded Cage before that first night. I was certain of that. Aside from the fact that I would have recognized her prior to the masquerade, I'd seen the innocence in her eyes when she walked into that room with me. She hadn't been a virgin, and she hadn't been completely unaware of what the point of the room had been, but she was a newcomer to the life, that much had been clear.

Was I supposed to think it had been a coincidence that she'd come to see me, and then shown up at the club and come straight to me? I wasn't an idiot. She had to have known, somehow, that I would be there. Had to have recognized me. It couldn't have been random, and I refused to believe it was something like destiny or some shit like that. That kind of fantasy wasn't real. Instant lust, sure. I could agree to that. Hell, I'd been attracted to Savannah from that first moment. Maybe she picked up on that and then somehow figured out where I would be.

It wasn't cynical, to think that she'd gone to the club to look for me, to dig up dirt that she could use in her article. My friends and I had chosen Gilded Cage for its discretion. People were more accepting of this sort of thing, but none of the four of us wanted to be pushed into the limelight. We understood the importance of media, but that didn't mean we wanted to see our personal lives splashed all over it. *The Heart of Art* liked to regard itself as above tawdry celebrity news that other publications promoted, but they still had to get people to buy their magazine, and some salacious details would do that.

I never should have agreed to do the fucking interview in the first place. I'd never done more than answer a couple questions before, but I'd agreed to do this show to raise awareness and funds for a great cause, which meant I couldn't simply fly below the radar. So, I'd agreed to talk to the press, to do what I could to promote both the show and the sponsoring charity.

But I hadn't seen Savannah coming. Not as a reporter, and certainly not as a lover.

No. She wasn't a lover.

Just someone I had sex with twice.

Even if she didn't have any ulterior motives, that's all she'd ever be. And I still didn't believe that she was innocent in all this.

I had to know.

It was that thought that got me out of bed. As I showered, I thought out exactly how I was going to find the truth. I knew her magazine was legitimate, and I didn't doubt for a moment that she really had been assigned to write a story on me and a critique on the show. Which meant I didn't need to dig into that, but rather look into who she was talking to and what she'd learned about me.

My first calls after I dressed were to the guys. I didn't think they'd be spilling any of my secrets, but I'd told them about the interview, so if Savannah had spoken with them, they probably wouldn't have completely blown her off.

Except all three of them said they hadn't answered any questions for anyone about me.

So, if she wasn't talking to them, she had to be doing some digging elsewhere. And I knew of at least one person who'd be more than willing to tell all for whatever cash offered.

Fuck.

I had to call my mother.

The phone rang twice before she picked up. "Jace? Sweetie?"

I closed my eyes and mentally cursed Savannah for one more thing to make my day suck. "Hi, Mom."

"I haven't heard from you in ages, sweetie. Is everything okay?"

I almost laughed. She was the last person I'd go to if things were bad. Well, maybe next-to-last. I wasn't calling her because I needed a shoulder to cry on – *that* would never happen.

"I'm doing a show." I wasn't about to do the small talk, pretend we're a real mother and son thing. "For charity, so I'm not getting any money for anything."

"I'd love to come–"

"That's not why I called." I closed my eyes, unable to imagine seeing her again. "There's a reporter who's writing a piece about me and I was wondering if she got in touch with you."

Silence for several long seconds, and I could almost hear the wheels in her head turning.

"I'm sure you don't want the past taking away from everything you're trying to accomplish."

It didn't take a genius to know where she was going with this. In fact, considering my mother's history, an idiot would've been able to figure out what she wanted.

"Has she talked to you or not?"

"No." She sounded almost disappointed.

"If she does, let me know." I gritted my teeth. "Maybe the two of us could discuss it over dinner some time."

"That would be wonderful." The cheery note in her voice told me that she knew exactly what I'd offer her if she kept her mouth shut.

"Thanks, Mom." I quickly continued before she could start talking again, "I have to go, but don't forget to contact me if someone calls asking questions."

I hung up as soon as she agreed and let out a breath. As far as conversations with my mother went, that one actually hadn't been that bad. It was possible that Savannah wouldn't be able to find the woman who had given me life but little else. There'd been more than a few years where I'd gone almost eighteen months or more without knowing where she was.

There was one other person I knew who wouldn't think twice about spilling everything she knew about me...including the fact that I went to Gilded Cage. And she was the only person I knew of who I wanted to talk to less than my mother.

I didn't have her number in my phone, but I didn't need it. I'd dialed it often enough that my fingers still remembered the pattern, even when I wished they didn't.

"I wondered when you'd be calling." Bianca was practically purring when she answered. "I knew you couldn't stay away."

I was glad she couldn't see the look of distaste on my face at the thought of going back to her. No matter how pissed I was at Savannah, I wouldn't let it drive me back into Bianca's arms. I couldn't, however, handle the situation as bluntly as I wanted. I needed to keep Bianca on the phone long enough to find out what I needed to know.

So I ignored her comments and went straight to the point. "Since you've been back, has anyone been asking questions about me? About our prior relationship?"

I could almost hear her smile.

"Why, Jay, have you gone and gotten yourself into trouble? I told you no good would come of your sexual...preferences. Did you beat some poor, unsuspecting girl and she didn't enjoy it?"

As if Bianca hadn't already been involved in the life when we met. I closed my eyes and reminded myself that blowing up at Bianca would just make matters worse. "You and I both know that's not how things work." I let out a slow breath. "But that's not why I called. With this show coming up, I want all of the focus to be on the cause rather than on anything a reporter might dig up. Has anyone contacted you?"

When she took a moment to answer, I was struck by how similar Bianca and my mother were, and how much of an idiot I'd been for dating someone so vapid and shallow.

"There was someone in the lobby of my building yesterday who chatted me up about local artists. When I said I knew you, she seemed really interested."

Shit.

"What did you tell her?" I had to force the question to come out far less harshly than I wanted.

"Nothing, of course." Bianca sounded offended, but I knew her well enough to know how much she was enjoying this. "She was bound and determined to get me to talk though, so I doubt she gave up. I wouldn't be surprised if she showed up at your studio, or even the club."

My back stiffened. "Did you tell her about the club?"

"I don't think so, but she was persistent. I couldn't say that she hasn't found out about it on her own. I'd watch yourself, if I were you. Or maybe just avoid the club for a while until she gets tired of trying to track you down."

Fuck.

I barely heard anything else Bianca said, unable to stop all of the negative emotions inside me from boiling into a fury. I shouldn't have been surprised that Savannah had used me like that. Very few people weren't out for only themselves. I thought she was different, and it was that mistake that made my hands clench.

I wasn't going to take this quietly. Come Monday morning, I'd make sure she never fucked with me again.

SEVENTEEN
SAVANNAH

Even though I'd taken extra time this morning to put on more make-up than I usually wore, I still arrived early at work. The bags under my eyes I'd needed to cover had been earned through a sleepless weekend that I feared would lead into a sleepless week. One more night like that and I doubted any amount of concealer would disguise how exhausted I was.

I was already trying to figure out how to stay under Abel's radar through the day when I dropped my purse on my desk. No one else was in yet, but I could hear voices coming from the back. Since the only office back there was Abel's, I figured avoidance was the best policy...until I recognized the second voice.

Jace.

My heart skipped a beat. He was here.

No.

I shook my head. It didn't matter that he was here. He'd been a total ass to me. I didn't think I was blameless, but I definitely didn't deserve to be accused of using him for a story. Certainly not after I'd told him how much his art had meant to me.

Bastard.

But that didn't stop me from taking a step toward the back, toward *him*. Despite everything he said to me, I still craved his touch. But that was just my body. My brain knew better.

"I mean it," Jace's voice was hard. "Don't make me call my lawyer."

And before I could do bolt or hide, he was coming out of Abel's office, straight toward me. I knew he saw me because I was only a couple feet away, but he didn't even look my way. Only walked by without even acknowledging that I existed.

It shouldn't have hurt to see him go like that. We weren't together. Never had been. We'd had two nights of incredible sex, and that had been one night too many. I always learned from my mistakes, so from here on out, it'd be nothing but professional between the two of us. After his show, I'd never have to see or think of Jace Randall again.

"Savannah!" Abel barked as he stuck his head out of his office. "Get your ass in here!"

What the hell? My boss had always been a jerk, but that seemed to go above and beyond.

Still, I went. I liked having a job that was at least in the ballpark of what I wanted to do. More to the point, I liked it until I found something better.

Abel was sitting behind his desk, hands folded on top of his ample belly, face red. He jerked his chin toward the chair on the other side of his desk, his eyes narrowing behind his glasses. The scowl on his face deepened as I sat down.

"You're off the Randall story."

My jaw dropped for a few seconds before I snapped it shut. I waited for him to explain, and I knew he would. Not because he'd feel like I deserved to know, but because he'd want to make sure I knew exactly what I'd done wrong.

"I never should have given you the story to begin with, but I figured no one can screw up an art show for a locally established artist. A little online research, then go critique some pretentious 'new' art that any idiot with a bachelor's degree could write about."

My nails dug into my palms, and I reminded myself that it wouldn't be prudent to insult my boss. Especially not when he wasn't quite finished.

"But somehow, you managed to be unprofessional enough that Mr. Randall felt he had to come down and tell me that he wanted you to stay away from him."

"Unprofessional?" I practically sputtered the word. Jace had the gall to call me unprofessional? What the *fuck*?!

"He didn't go into any details, but you need to know that you won't be going on any assignments for a hell of a long time. You're going to be staying here. Getting coffee. Maybe, if you're lucky, I'll let you do some fact checking." Abel pointed toward the door. "Get back to your desk and send me everything you have so far. I'll take the story from here."

Like hell he would.

But I wasn't going to argue that now. I needed to get my shit together first. Calm down so that I didn't go off on Abel or Jace. I needed to think, figure things out logically. Cooler heads prevailed in the end, and right now, I wasn't certain that I could say anything without losing the tenuous grip I had on my self-control. Inhaling deeply, I simply stood and walked out of the office. My hands were shaking, my stomach churning. Emotions flashed through me, one right after the other, too fast for me to process. All I knew for certain was that as quickly as I'd thought my career was finally taking off, I was now just as certain that it was over.

EIGHTEEN
SAVANNAH

Today had been about as much fun as...honestly, there were very few things I could think of that sucked as much as today had. Root canal. Pap smear. Pretty much any medical procedure. That time in eighth grade when I got my period in the middle of English and didn't realize it until Abbie Jamison started laughing. Or when I was seventeen, and Everett was looking in my room for something and found the vibrator I'd just bought but hadn't yet dared to use.

It was too hot to walk, and I didn't feel like taking the subway, so as soon as I stepped outside, I flagged down a taxi. Fortunately, I'd managed to get out ahead of the rush and only had to wait a minute or so. As soon as I was inside the cab, I pulled out my phone and sent a group text. I needed reinforcements before I did something crazy.

Like going straight to Jace's house and demanding to know where he got off being such a fucking jackass.

Not a good idea. Not a good idea.

I kept repeating that to myself as I waited for my friends to text back. I breathed a sigh of relief as first one, then the rest, responded. Everett was already home, and the girls would meet us at our favorite restaurant in a couple hours. This was why I loved them. I hadn't told them anything other than I needed them, and they said they'd be there.

When I got home, Everett didn't try to get anything out of me, but the grim expression on his face told me that I only needed to say the word and he'd do whatever I asked.

I changed into something nice but comfortable. Not sexy. I wasn't going out with my friends to dance and find someone to fuck. I'd never felt less like having sex than I did right now. All I wanted to do was vent to them and then let them distract me for the rest of the night. I still had to go to work tomorrow, and the day after that, which meant I needed to figure out how to deal with things, but for tonight, I needed the break.

"You look nice," Everett said as we headed downstairs.

"Thanks." I reached for his hand, appreciating the familiar feeling. "So do you."

He pulled me against his side with one arm and waved down a taxi with his free hand. "Whatever you need tonight, Sav. We've got you."

"LET ME GET THIS STRAIGHT," Lorde said as she leaned forward, blue-green eyes flashing, "you suggest that the two of you reveal your identities *before* you have sex, but he says he wants to do it after, then blames you for not telling him who you were sooner?"

"And then he goes to your boss and complains, getting you removed from the story," Everett finished, the muscle in his jaw popping with each word.

"That about sums it up." I stabbed a piece of steak with my fork, then glared at it.

"Fuck him." Lei put her hand on my arm, squeezing gently. "He deserves to get some second-rate hack writing about him and his show."

I dropped my fork, wincing as it clattered against the plate. "It's for a great cause though. Clean drinking water." I sighed and press my fingers against my temples. "I can't really bring myself to wish for the show to crash and burn when that's what he's doing it for."

"I can," Lei said doggedly.

"So can I." Lorde's normally bubbly voice filled with an anger I wasn't used to seeing from her. "And I'll ask Robert to look into donating to charities that provide something similar, so you don't have to feel bad about wanting that jerk to fail."

I gave them both a watery smile. This was exactly why

I called them. I was a strong, independent person, but that didn't mean it wasn't nice to have some support once in a while. Especially when it came to dealing with the extra sensitive shit I couldn't call home about.

I loved my parents and my brother, but there was no way in hell I'd talk to them about anything relating to sex, even the vanilla kind. They weren't naive enough to think that I wasn't having it, but we didn't talk about that sort of thing in my family. The sex talk my mom had given me when I was ten had been all flat-out biology and anatomy, and even that had embarrassed the hell out of her.

"Maybe you should start putting in applications elsewhere," Lorde suggested. "I mean, it's not like *The Heart of Art* is the *Times* or anything."

"I know." I dropped my face in my hands and groaned. "And it's not even that I really like the magazine, but it's one of the few art magazines still in print. It'd be nice to have that on my resumé before I go somewhere else."

"Everything's digital now. Why fight it?" Lei reached across the table and stole a crouton off my salad. "If I could work from home in my pajamas, I'd do it."

I nodded, but my heart wasn't in it. I knew she had a good point, and there was some appeal in working from home, but I always imagined myself working in an office where I was part of a group dedicated to bringing news to its readers in physical print that I could cut out and mail home to my parents. Like a female art critic version of Clark Kent.

I closed my eyes and rubbed my temples. Maybe this was life's way of telling me that I wasn't as logical and pragmatic as I liked to think. That perhaps I had a more romanticized version of how I thought my life was supposed to go than I wanted to admit.

Dammit! I didn't want to be that person. The one who had this vision of how things were supposed to go and then freaked out when they didn't follow that plan. I was smarter than that. I didn't follow my heart. I followed my head.

And the one time I hadn't, the one time I'd let myself hope that I could have something more than just a night or two of hot sex, I'd been reminded none too kindly that wasn't the way things worked.

"Hey, we've got your back." Everett put his hand on the back of my neck and gave it a comforting squeeze. "I'll go kick his ass if you want me to."

I was sorely tempted to take him up on it. If anyone could take on Jace, it would be Everett. But I didn't want to risk my best friend getting hurt. I told myself that I didn't care whether or not Everett hurt Jace, but I wasn't *that* good of a liar.

"No," I said reluctantly. "It's probably best for everyone if we go our separate ways."

"I think you're right." Lorde grasped my hand. "At least

New York's a huge city, so the chances of the two of you running into each other again are slim."

I was about to agree with her, except at that moment, I heard a commotion coming from the front of the restaurant and turned to see four insanely attractive men being led to a nearby table. I recognized one as being Reb Union, a musician I really liked, and two I didn't know. The fourth, of course, was Jace.

Fate sucked.

"Dammit," I muttered, barely able to get the word out past the emotion clogging my throat.

"Sav?" Lorde's fingers tightened around mine. "What's wrong?"

It took far too much self-control not to look again as I said, "That's him. With the group that just arrived."

"Him who?" Lei asked. Her voice took on an edge. "That asshole? Where?"

"The group of really hot guys?" Lorde asked, her eyes wide. "With Reb Union?"

I nodded.

All three let out low whistles, and I couldn't blame them. Those were probably four of the best-looking men I'd ever seen, and I spent my life being friends with Everett.

"Which one is he?" Everett's voice was harder than I'd ever heard it. "Which of those guys is he, Savannah?"

"The blond," I mumbled as I stared down at my hands.

The really hot one with the sexy tattoos who's great with his hands.

A muscled arm wrapped around my shoulders and pulled me over. I ducked my head against Everett's shoulder and let him hug me. Except he didn't let me go after a couple minutes like he usually did.

I raised my head. "What are you doing, Ev?"

He grinned, but there was a bit of steel behind his eyes. "I'm being a good boyfriend."

I started to roll my eyes, but when he raised an eyebrow, I realized he was serious. He knew how upset I was, how shitty I'd been treated, and he wasn't going to let Jace get away with thinking that he'd hurt me.

Everett pressed a kiss to my forehead. "I'm serious, Sav. Let me play the part and show that bastard that he lost the best thing that could've ever happened to him."

It was appealing, I had to admit. Flirt and cuddle with Everett so that Jace could see that what he'd done hadn't destroyed me, that I wouldn't be spending my time mooning over him like some lovestruck schoolgirl.

But was that really how I wanted to play things? I wasn't sure.

NINETEEN
JACE

The girl who'd gotten Alix all tied up in knots had been gone for like two weeks, but he still looked like shit. I knew Erik was worried about his cousin, and any other time, I would've been right there with him. Hell, I *knew* I should've been with him and Reb when it came to trying to cheer up our friend, but another part of me wanted to side with Alix, to tell him it was okay to brood.

I'd been so sure I was in the right that when I stormed into Abel Updike's office, I'd been all righteous anger. I hadn't thought twice about threatening that smarmy little man with a lawsuit if he didn't immediately take Savannah off the story and assign it to someone else. I didn't want her anywhere near me or my show.

Except when I'd stepped outside the office and she'd been there, all of the anger inside me had burned away, and I'd known that if I looked at her even once, I'd have been lost. Because deep down in my gut, I knew I hadn't been fair to her.

"Jace." Reb elbowed me right before I walked into a wall. "Pay attention."

"Sorry." I scrubbed my hand over my face. "Long day."

I needed tonight with my friends as much as Alix did. We'd chosen a restaurant over a club, but a beer – or three – was definitely in my future.

And then I heard a familiar laugh. For a moment, I froze, sure I had to have been mistaken. But then I saw her out of the corner of my eye and wondered how in the world I could have not seen that she and my masked woman were the same. I'd know her anywhere, no matter how painful it was.

And seeing a tall, attractive man with his arm around her was definitely more painful than it should have been.

I forced myself not to look directly at her, but I couldn't stop myself from sneaking a peek as we walked by. She was with two other women as well, but it was the guy who had my attention.

I didn't like him.

"You're not looking so hot," Alix said as he plopped down in the seat next to me.

"Right back at you," I snapped. "I'm in the mood for something harder than a beer. What about you?"

"Talisker," he ordered the moment the waiter appeared. "A lot of it."

"So..." Erik launched into some story that I didn't particularly care about, and wasn't nearly distracting enough.

She was laughing again. Dammit. I couldn't do this. I sighed, then leaned back so that I could actually see her.

That blond douche had his hand in her hair, raking his fingers through silky curls before tracing a finger along her jaw. It wasn't just that he was touching her that irked me. It was the fact that he seemed so relaxed about it. Like it was his fucking right.

It wasn't that *I* wanted to touch her, of course. Just that I didn't think she'd appreciate being manhandled in public.

I was only looking out for her.

Except that didn't explain why my hands kept clenching, or the churning in my stomach.

Or why I couldn't stop myself from looking over at her constantly, needing to see what she was doing, if she was smiling. That was what I didn't understand. How could she be smiling after what happened? I'd gone off on her, then sabotaged her career. Hell, I'd be seriously pissed if she done something like that to me. But she seemed to barely care. Did that mean she didn't care about her job? That didn't really mesh with the woman I met, but now I wondered if anything about her had been real at all.

"What the hell's up with you?" Reb asked as he

motioned for the waiter to bring us another round. "You look constipated."

"Shut up, jackass." I punched his shoulder harder than I probably should have. "You're one to talk. You look like shit."

He gave me a one-shouldered shrug. "Yeah, well...bite me."

"Eloquent, Reb. Really."

As he picked up his now-full glass, he used his free hand to flip me off.

"Jay, sweetheart!"

Dammit. This seriously couldn't be happening.

I hadn't seen her at all in four years, and now I couldn't get away from her.

Just as I opened my mouth to tell her that I was busy with my friends, I saw something out of the corner of my eye that made me instantly do a one-eighty.

Savannah was watching.

I used my foot to push out the empty chair next to me and watched as Bianca artfully draped herself in it. As always, every move was made to draw as much attention as possible. I wasn't particularly interested, but I made myself look at her legs as she crossed them, at her breasts as she folded her arms in a way that pushed up her cleavage.

"Ready to admit how much you missed me?" The toe of her shoe ran up the inside of my calf.

I raised an eyebrow and ignored Reb muttering unflattering things under his breath. My friends hadn't liked Bianca any more than we'd liked Reb's ex. That was okay though. I wasn't inviting her to become a part of my life again, just letting her distract me. I didn't care much how she did it.

Before the main meal arrived, she was sitting as close as possible to me, her thigh pressed against mine, her arm across the back of my chair. Her fingers raked through the back of my hair, nails scratching my scalp hard enough to sting. I knew what she was trying to do, but it wasn't working. I could appreciate that she was beautiful, but I felt no attraction to her. Hell, my cock didn't even twitch when she put her lips against my ear.

Her words, however, made the rest of me sit up and pay attention.

"So, is that woman over there, the one you can't take your eyes off of, the reporter I'm supposed to watch out for?"

TWENTY
SAVANNAH

I wasn't really sure when I made the decision to take Everett up on his offer, only that it had been easy to lean into him, to let his touch linger. I didn't feel anything more than the same friendly, platonic warmth I'd always felt for him, but it'd been nice. So I'd let him flirt and joke and tease, and I'd gone along with it.

And then a pretty, curvy woman with perfect chocolate skin sauntered over to Jace and started some very *un*-platonic flirting.

It shouldn't have hurt to see him letting her run her hands over his neck and shoulders, whispering sweet nothings in his ear. The fact that she was practically sitting on his lap shouldn't have made me wonder when they'd met, if they'd already fucked, when they would fuck again.

And it shouldn't have made me angry enough to move from where I was sitting to Everett's lap.

He gave me a startled look but didn't hesitate to wrap his arms around my waist. He put his face close to mine so that he could speak without anyone else hearing. "Sav, sweetheart, I don't think this is the sort of place where a lap dance is entirely appropriate."

I laughed and kissed his cheek before moving back to my own seat. Everett had gotten the message though and put his arm around me. I'd never thought of myself as a petty person, but I couldn't deny that I enjoyed knowing that if Jace looked over here, he'd see me with an attentive, smoking hot man...and not thinking about him at all.

And it worked, made me feel better.

Until I looked over and saw the woman with her hand in Jace's lap under the table.

"Excuse me," I mumbled as I jumped up. "I need to use the restroom."

I doubted my friends believed me, but I didn't wait around to explain. Heat flooded my face as I hurried toward the back of the restaurant. I'd been an idiot to think that this was a good idea. The moment I'd seen Jace come in, I should have told my friends I wanted to leave. I wasn't a woman who normally played games, and I shouldn't have tried to change that.

After I washed my hands, I splashed cold water on my face, then patted it dry, grateful that my make-up was waterproof. It'd be bad enough to go out there with flushed cheeks. Looking like a raccoon was completely unacceptable.

I automatically glanced up when I heard the door open, and then immediately wished I hadn't when I saw the dark-haired beauty who'd been hanging all over Jace. I turned my attention back to drying my hands and hoped she didn't catch the fact that I'd been staring for a few seconds before I caught myself.

Heels clicked on the tiles as she came closer, and I realized that things were about to get awkward as I tried to explain why I'd been looking at her. I took a slow breath, fixed what I hoped was an adequate smile on my face, and straightened. As I turned toward her, I opened my mouth to apologize, but only got out the first syllable before she interrupted.

"I know who you are."

Shit.

I had two choices, and neither one was appealing since they both required I stay where I was rather than run away. I could play dumb and pretend that I had no idea what she was talking about, or I could own up to everything and hope that she wasn't Jace's girlfriend.

"I think it's tacky that you'd follow Jace here," she continued. "But he's too polite to tell you to fuck off, so I figured I'd do it for him."

My jaw dropped. That hadn't been the angle I thought she'd play. "It's not like–"

"Look," she cut me off again, "I get that he's probably the best sex you've ever had, but you should know that he only fucked you to make sure you gave him a good review."

I flinched as her words hit me, but before I could take them to heart, logic piped up. I squared my shoulders. "If that's true, why did he get me thrown off the story? Seems to me, if he only slept with me so I'd give him a good review, he would've wanted to stay in my good graces. Getting me demoted wasn't really the best way to do that."

The woman's eyes narrowed, but she didn't miss a beat. "Because I came back. Jace wanted me. He *always* wants me. And he didn't want to wait until the show was over to have me. I always come before his little hobby."

I felt a flicker of anger at her referring to Jace's art as a hobby, but then remembered how he treated me and pushed it aside. I still wasn't going to accept this woman's version of how things had gone though. I could accept that he'd been angry with me for not telling him as soon as I realized who he was, and I could even understand why he'd think I might spill his secrets, but seducing me for a good review then breaking things off in such a humiliating manner didn't seem to be Jace's style. I might have misjudged him, but I doubted I'd done so that much. He could have walked away without making it personal, and gotten both a good review and still been with this woman.

"Why'd he fuck me the second time, then?" I asked, crossing my arm over my chest. "If he was in such an all-fired hurry to get back to you, why didn't he just break things off and walk away the moment he saw me?"

Something flickered across her eyes and her mouth tightened. I almost thought I'd struck a nerve by giving her something she couldn't explain away, but then she shrugged.

"You threw yourself at him, so he gave you a pity fuck. I don't know many men who'd turn down free pussy, no matter how bad you are at sex."

I sucked in a breath as the barb went deep. Was that what happened? Had I been so desperate to have sex with him again that I convinced myself that he wanted me when all he'd seen was an easy fuck?

I clenched my jaw to keep back the tears burning my eyes and stepped around the woman. As soon as I was out of the bathroom, I headed straight for the exit. I couldn't stay, not even with Everett there next to me, pretending to be my boyfriend.

The evening air was hot and muggy, thick with all the scents of the city, but I gulped in deep breaths all the same, willing the warmth to calm my fragile nerves. I needed to get myself together before I hailed a cab.

"Savannah, what's wrong?" Lei asked from behind me.

I turned to see all three of my friends standing there, wearing nearly identical expressions of concern on their faces. Lorde wrapped her arms around me while Everett and Lei transitioned from concerned to pissed.

"What happened?" Everett asked. "Did that asshole–"

I held up a hand. "He didn't do...he didn't say anything."

Lei's eyes narrowed. "Spill it, Sav."

They clearly weren't going to let me go home until I told them, so I just blurted out what happened. All of it. Pretty much verbatim. And then I leaned back against the wall and covered my face with my hands, pretending that none of this ever happened.

TWENTY-ONE
JACE

By the time Bianca came back from the restroom, Erik was eager to get back to Tanya, and Reb wanted to take Alix somewhere to get some harder alcohol. Since I wasn't about to get stuck at the table with just Bianca, I told the guys I was going to the bathroom before heading out, then said a quick goodbye to her as I passed. Maybe it was the coward's way out, but I wasn't feeling particularly brave or chivalrous at the moment.

"Where the *fuck* do you get off, you self-centered bastard?!"

I blinked down at the petite Japanese-American girl glaring up at me. She poked me in the chest to make sure I had no misconceptions about who she was talking to. It still didn't tell me who she was though...and then it hit me. She was one of the women who'd been sitting with Savannah.

Shit.

"How dare you use my friend like that? You sleep with her, so she'll give you a good review, and then when some old piece of ass shows up, you can't even walk away like a decent person? You had to humiliate her and get her demoted?"

I shook my head and held up a hand, confused. "What the hell are you talking about?"

The woman's eyes narrowed to a scary degree. "That tramp you had hanging all over you told Savannah everything."

My stomach twisted painfully. "I'm going to need you to slow down and explain exactly what it is you think I did."

The girl crossed her arms, the expression on her face almost making me take a step back. "Why? You didn't give Savannah a chance to explain anything before you jumped to conclusions and tried to ruin her life. So why shouldn't I believe what your *friend* said?"

"Bianca's not my friend." I wasn't sure why that was important for me to make that clear before I addressed anything else. "What exactly did she say? And to who?"

She seemed to be considering whether or not to slap me and walk away, or actually answer my question. "Savannah. Your *Bianca bitch* told Savannah that you only slept with her to get a good review for your show."

What the total fuck?

"That's not...shit." I closed my eyes for a moment as the events of the last few days replayed in my mind rapid-fire, each and every mistake I'd made showing up in glaring technicolor. "Savannah really didn't know who I was the first time we were together, did she?"

"No."

A sharp nail dug into my chest again, and I opened my eyes to see a look of pure disgust on the young woman's face.

"And she'd never tell anyone the sordid little details of what you did either. She didn't even tell us. Just that the two of you met at a club and hooked up. We're not idiots. We know when she's lying or hiding something. But we also know that she would only do that for a good reason." Even as the guilt dug in its claws, Savannah's friend put her hands on her hips. "I have no clue why she'd keep things from us for you. You don't look like you're worth it."

The sad thing was, as she walked away, I wasn't entirely sure I disagreed with her.

I needed to find Savannah.

I turned and rushed toward the entrance, fully expecting to have to find a taxi. Except, as soon as I stepped outside, I remembered that I didn't know where she lived. I turned, now at a loss of what to do next, but then I saw someone familiar. The tall, good-looking blond man who'd had his hands on Savannah.

I took two steps toward him, then realized that he and

the other woman from Savannah's table were both holding on to someone.

Savannah.

Knowing that I could quite possibly get a broken nose for what I was about to do didn't stop me from doing it. I owed her the risk at the very least.

"Savannah?" Three pairs of eyes looked at me, and I wasn't sure which set was more pissed. "Can I have a word with you?"

"Arrogant little–" The man took a step in my direction, but Savannah put her hand on his chest, a gesture of familiarity that made my stomach twist.

"Everett." Her voice was quiet. "It's okay. Let me talk to him." She looked up at him. "I'll meet you at home."

Home? Jealousy was a bright, hot lance through me. Why had I come out here to apologize to her for the misunderstanding between us if she'd been living with some guy this whole time? And there was no way in hell he was her brother. Brothers didn't touch their sisters like he'd been touching her.

Still, I'd made a mess of things before because I made an assumption rather than talking things out. I'd say what I came here to say, then I'd listen to her. After I heard her out, I'd decide what I should do from that point.

Everett and the unnamed woman walked away, shooting me angry looks as they went back inside. Before I could say anything else, Savannah gestured for me to follow her. We moved around the side of the building to a small and surprisingly clean alley. Half a dozen bicycles were locked up near a door that I suspected led into the kitchen or back room of the restaurant, but I doubted we'd be interrupted. The place had been packed.

When we were sufficiently hidden in the shadows, she turned back toward me.

I'd fucked things up with her – badly – and I didn't know if it was too late to fix it, but I had to at least try, and part of that meant I wasn't going to attempt to justify my previous behavior.

"I'm sorry."

She folded her arms and raised an eyebrow as if she were waiting for more.

Fair enough.

"When I realized who you were...I didn't...dammit." I cursed as I ran my hand through my hair. Where was I supposed to begin to explain so she could see the difference between what I was apologizing for and what I hadn't done at all?

"Start at the beginning," she suggested.

I nodded. "I didn't know it was you, that first night at the club. Or the second night. Not until you took off your mask. I didn't use you." I took a step toward her, needing her to be able to look into my eyes and see the truth of each word. "I swear, Savannah, I know I acted like a total ass, but those things Bianca said to you weren't true."

Some of the tension on her face eased, and I saw a flare of hope in her eyes for a brief moment before she extinguished it. I hadn't let myself admit just how much she meant to me until I realized I was the one in the wrong. Every single thing I thought she'd done had been a reason for me to ignore the attraction I felt, and now that those were out of the way, I could finally accept just how much I wanted her.

"I am so sorry." I started to reach for her, then dropped my hand, not knowing if she wanted me to touch her. "For what I said, and for what I did. I promise that I'll go straight to your boss first thing tomorrow and fix it. I'll tell him it was entirely on me. Temperamental artist shit. None of it was your fault and that I'll only agree to having an interview published if you're the one to do it."

Her eyes had an almost unnatural glow in the dim lighting. "I'm sorry I didn't tell you as soon as I realized what happened. I shouldn't have let it go as far as it did while you were in the dark."

"I appreciate that," I said sincerely. "But I know it still doesn't excuse what I said or did." A moment of silence fell between us, and then I had to ask, "If you need to get back to your boyfriend–"

"Roommate," she said with a smile. "And before you ask, he's gay."

Relief flooded me, but I tried not to let it show. "He certainly wasn't acting like he was gay."

She laughed. "He was trying to help me by making you think that I'd moved on."

I wanted to ask her if she had moved on, but I chose another question instead. "Do you remember what happened the first time we met?" I dared to close the distance between us, my heart thudding against my ribs when she didn't move away. "How we had that misunderstanding?"

The corners of her mouth twitched upward in a partial smile. "I remember. I thought you were insinuating I was a prostitute, and you seemed to think I was an incompetent food delivery person."

I laughed. God, it felt good to laugh, even if it was a small burst of sound. "We moved past it. I know what I did the other day was so much worse, but I'm hoping you can forgive me."

"Why?" she asked. "Why do you want me to forgive you?"

I didn't stop myself from reaching out this time, letting my thumb slide along her jaw before burying my hand in those silky curls. "Because I've wanted you from the moment I saw you across the club, and even when I was furious at you, I wanted you."

Even in the imperfect light of the alley, her pale eyes darkened. "I wanted you too."

I cupped the back of her head as I lowered my mouth to hers, stopping just short of kissing her. "I still want you...but I understand if you don't–"

"I want you too." Even as she breathed the last word, she closed the distance between us.

I couldn't stop myself from moaning the moment our lips touched. I'd almost forgotten how soft her skin was, the taste of her mouth. It was the first time we'd kissed without masks, the first time I'd known exactly who it was I was kissing. And I wanted more.

She bit my bottom lip, then sucked it into her mouth, sending the blood rushing from my brain straight to my cock. Her boldness didn't surprise me. With the mask and without it, she was the same woman. Confident. Willing and able to claim what she wanted. I suspected the only reason the mask had appealed to her was because the Gilded Cage was a new experience.

I pressed her back against the wall, running my hands down her sides to her hips, feeling the strength in her slight body. She looked so delicate, so easy to break, but I remembered all too well how it had felt to be inside her, to take her hard and fast. I knew that she craved what I had to offer, the things I had promised her.

"Fuck, Savannah," I groaned as I tore my lips from hers. "I can't control myself with you."

She reached down between us, fingers quickly working

my pants open. I cursed again as her hand wrapped around my cock, gritting my teeth as I grabbed her wrist.

"Like I said," I locked eyes with her, "control seems to be an issue when I'm around you."

The smile that curved her lips could only be called wicked. "Why don't you do something about it then?"

My surprise lasted only a few seconds as I read the challenge in her eyes. I glanced up the alley, but none of the people passing by sent even a glance in our direction.

"Do you want me to take you right here?" I asked, my voice rough as I pulled her hand from my pants. I stretched her arms above her head, pinning them to the wall. "Think about your answer, because if you say yes, I'm not going to be gentle."

She rocked her hips against me. "I don't want you to be."

I didn't give her a chance to second-guess herself. I'd stop if she told me to, but if she didn't...

I pulled back far enough to turn her around. She made a breathless sound as her hands went out automatically to brace herself against the wall. I yanked her pants down, exposing her pale, translucent skin. I knew we had to be quick, but I couldn't stop myself from stopping for a moment and sinking my teeth into the firm flesh of her ass.

She let out a yelp, glaring over her shoulder at me. I kissed the mark I'd left, then straightened.

"I'm clean," I said as I slipped my hand between her legs. She gasped as I found her slick and hot. "Are you safe?"

She nodded. "Please, Jace."

I put my mouth against her ear even as I slid the head of my cock against her entrance. "I'll have you begging me for real soon enough."

She cried out as I drove into her, burying myself in a single thrust. I clamped my hand over her mouth and felt a shiver pass through her. Fuck. The position made her even tighter, and I knew I wouldn't last long, but I'd be damned if I couldn't get her off before I did.

Fortunately, she wasn't the sort of woman who needed soft and gentle to climax.

I stroked her clit in tight circles as I made short, deep thrusts, each one driving me closer to the edge.

"I'm going to need you to come for me," I said between harsh breaths. "I need to feel you come apart on my cock."

Her tongue flicked out against my palm, and I groaned, pressing my face against the place where her neck met her shoulder. I worried her skin between my teeth, marking her in a place where others could see and know that she was taken. For as long as this fire burned between us, she was *mine.*

The thought tipped me over, and as I emptied inside her, I pressed my fingers harder against her clit. "Come,

Savannah." I made it an order. "Come for me now, and I'll spend the rest of the night making you scream my name."

As she shattered in my arms, I promised myself that I would make good on my word, and I'd make sure she didn't regret forgiving me.

TWENTY-TWO
SAVANNAH

It had been nearly three weeks since Jace apologized for what he'd done and said. Three weeks since he'd taken me from behind in an alley and made me come hard enough to see stars. Three weeks since I'd had to listen to Everett, Lei, and Lorde all telling me why I was making a mistake.

Three of the best weeks of my life.

Jace had gone straight to Abel the morning after we made up, and my article had been returned before lunch. My boss was still a bit of an ass, but at least my career was back on track. And with my...*exclusive* access to the artist, I had plenty of material to choose from.

As for how much material Jace now had to work with...

He'd only been sculpting for the show now, his paints and canvases put to the side. I'd seen him create a couple pieces, watched as those strong hands molded and formed various types of clay into beautiful works of art.

Works of art that bore a resemblance to various parts of my body. My hands. My face with the mask I'd worn the first night we were together.

It had been insanely erotic to watch him create, to mold and caress with those strong hands of his. Which was probably why those sessions had almost always turned into incredibly hot sex marathons. We'd fucked in his studio, living room, kitchen, pool house...pretty much everywhere except for his actual bedroom. When we needed a bed, we went to his 'playroom.' I didn't mind though. We hadn't discussed exactly what this was between us, who we were to each other, and spending the night in his bed seemed like the sort of thing that could wait until we'd had that talk.

Right now, I was happy with what we had.

In those long hours, I learned more about the things that could bring me pleasure than I had with any previous lover. And more about myself as well. Jace wasn't simply teaching me about what it meant to be a submissive. He was teaching me about how anticipation could make culmination even sweeter, how the right kind of pain could make an orgasm even more intense, how denial could draw out pleasure until it was nearly agony.

Even now, as I sat at my desk, the memories of our

times together warmed my skin and made me squirm in my chair.

Okay, so the squirming had more to do with the fact that my ass was still burning from his use of a flogger last night than it did from my memories. Both were responsible for how wet I was, and I knew if I didn't start thinking about something less erotic, I was going to need to slip into the bathroom on my lunch break and take care of myself.

Even though Jace had specifically forbidden me touching myself without his permission.

Which, of course, made it impossible to stop thinking about doing it.

It would be so easy, I knew, even here, to slide my hand under my skirt, to move aside my panties, and to slip my fingers between my folds. It wouldn't take much. Just the memories of the last few weeks and a few passes of my fingers over my clit.

Memories like three nights ago when Jace tied me up and showed me something he called wax play.

My skin tingled as my mind filled...

This was new.

All right, so technically, pretty much everything Jace had introduced me to was new, but this was new for us. Before, when he restrained me, he used handcuffs or similar things on my wrists, or if he wanted me completely tied up, he would spread me out on his bed until I was completely exposed.

Tonight, however, he had me kneel, legs apart, hands behind my back, head up. When I was positioned exactly how he wanted me, he brought out a set of soft leather straps and began to bind me. First, he wrapped cuffs around each wrist and ankle, then connected right wrist to right ankle, and the left side the same way. I shifted, testing each side as I catalogued how much motion I had. It wasn't much. Instead of restricting my side to side movement, it kept my arms behind me and my shoulders back, putting my breasts on display. And standing would be an impossibility until he released me. It wasn't exactly uncomfortable, but I was once again glad that Jace wasn't into tying me up and leaving me for long periods of time.

Then he brought over the candle, and a part of me wondered if this would be the place I finally drew a line. He gave me the same reassuring smile that he always did when we got to a point where my nerves were about to get the best of me. He never coerced me into anything I didn't want to do, but he did have a knack for soothing my worries until I decided to give him a chance. Granted, I hadn't regretted it yet.

"It's going to hurt," he said honestly. "But it's a special kind of wax, made specifically for this sort of thing, so it's safe."

I nodded, the butterflies still fluttering in my stomach. He cupped my chin and ran his thumb along my bottom lip. My eyes locked with his – a no-no for most subs, I now knew, but one he permitted for a reason he hadn't yet shared – and I flicked out my tongue against the tip of his thumb. Those jade eyes of his darkened to near-black and he cursed softly.

"The things you do to me," he murmured as he straightened. His posture changed, and I knew we were transitioning from reassurance to whatever it was he was going to do with that candle.

The first drops landed on the tops of my breasts, and I jerked at the sharp pain shooting across my nerves. It didn't last long, quickly turning into a tender burn, similar to what I felt when he spanked me or used a flogger. Not entirely unpleasant, but nothing I would have described as particularly pleasant *either.*

Not yet anyway.

If my time with Jace had taught me anything, it was that how things began wasn't always how things ended.

I gasped as another drop fell onto my breast, a little lower this time. I'd never minded my smaller bust, but as he dropped another bit of wax on my breast, I wish I was a bit bigger, if only to avoid the place I knew the hot liquid was going next.

His thumb moved over my hardened nipple, then up to brush across the hardened wax. My eyelids fluttered, and I leaned into his touch. He made a sound in the back of his throat and took a step back.

"I still don't have as much control around you as I

would like," he said quietly.

His admission warmed me in a whole different way. Before I could dwell on it too much though, he was tipping the candle again.

The next drop landed directly on my nipple, and I couldn't stop myself from crying out. But even as the pain burned through my sensitive skin, I could feel my pussy growing wet...

"Savannah?"

I jerked back to reality, flushing as I looked up to see Abel's secretary standing next to my desk. "Sorry, just lost in thought."

Kathy gave me a bored look that said she didn't really care. "Mr. Updike wants to know if you've spoken with Robby about when to do the pictures for the article."

Shit. I knew I'd forgotten something.

I reached for my phone. "I'll give him a call right now."

She sniffed as she walked away, making it clear exactly what she thought of my promise. I rolled my eyes and picked up my phone. I wasn't really that fond of our free-lance photographer, mostly because he loved to talk about his 'art' like the rest of us peons didn't understand what it truly meant to be an artist. Now that I thought about it, he and Abel were two of a kind, which made sense as to why Robby got away with coming to jobs looking like he hadn't showered or washed his clothes in a week.

He answered on the first ring and was surprisingly

pleasant as we discussed a schedule for the photos. I'd fully expected to have to argue to get him to go along with my vision for something that focused on the art rather than Jace, but for once, Robby readily agreed with everything I suggested.

Then I heard a girl giggling in the background and realized that he actually wanted to get me off the phone so he could get back to his company. I wasn't about to complain, not when I was going to hold him to everything he agreed to. As soon as we ended the call, I wrote everything up and sent it off to Abel to make sure it was locked in.

Once that was done, I pulled up the article and the outline I'd written and finished up the last of what I had to do until the show. Well, except the photos and captions. I still had those left. And any new pieces would need write-ups. I expected that it would have taken me longer if I hadn't had specific insight into the pieces Jace already had for display.

I managed to polish my work until it was time to leave, but before I could fill my head with thoughts of Jace and what we were going to do tonight, my phone rang. It wasn't a number I recognized, but I answered it anyway.

"Hello?"

"Savannah Birch?"

"Yes?"

The next words she spoke stopped me in my tracks.

TWENTY-THREE
JACE

I had a list. All the things I wanted to do with and to Savannah before this thing between us ended. Not that I was planning on breaking things off with her anytime soon. My list was too long for that. But it would happen soon enough. It always did. I'd enjoy my time with her, and then little by little, we'd want to spend more time apart. Any issues we ignored in the beginning would start to annoy us, and if we were lucky, we'd realize it was better to take a step back than to let things implode.

I enjoyed spending time with her before we started having sex, and if it was all possible, I wanted us to stay friends once everything else ended. I didn't want things between the two of us to become like they were between Bianca and me.

Which was another reason I always had to remember

that Savannah and I weren't dating. I'd learned my lesson from Bianca. I didn't do the whole boyfriend / girlfriend thing. Erik's relationship with Tanya was the exception, not the rule. I wasn't going to risk it. I didn't *want* to risk it.

There was only one risk worth taking, and that was the one that came with the cuffs and whips and other toys I possessed in my playroom. I'd enjoyed introducing those risks to Savannah. The sight of her stretched out and bound, her soft pink skin glistening with arousal, had tested my self-control in ways I never imagined. I'd tasted her, touched her, and it wasn't enough. Even when we weren't together, thoughts of her kept coming to me. How she sounded when I took her to the edge but kept her from falling over it. The look of her skin striped pink by my hand.

A few nights ago, I introduced her to wax play, and I could almost still feel the different sensations of her soft skin and the smooth heat of the wax. She made the sexiest sounds when the melted wax landed on her nipples. And an even hotter cry when I slid the first small ice cube into her pussy.

I closed my eyes and muttered a curse. Being with Savannah had opened up a part of my artistry that had been locked away for years, giving me the ability to focus better than I had in a long time. Of course, that didn't mean I wasn't occasionally interrupted by the need to take her again even in the middle of what I was working on.

I'd never been with a woman I craved so much. Even though I had plans for us tonight, I wasn't sure I could avoid fucking her at least once before we started our games. Just the thought of burying myself inside her was enough to make me hard.

"Jace?"

Her voice came from the front foyer a moment before the door closed behind her. I'd given her a spare key and the alarm code a month ago, so I didn't have to worry about being so caught up in my work that I left her standing outside in the summer heat.

"In here!"

I didn't wait for her to come to me though. All of my planning and my preparation had heated my blood too much. I caught her in the connecting corridor, my mouth coming down hard on hers. She wrapped her arms around my neck, and when I boosted her up, her legs went around my waist, her skirt pushing up past her hips. She made a sound in the back of her throat as she rocked against me, the friction nearly painful against my cock. I gripped her hair tight as I bit down on her bottom lip, but even though I knew both actions had to sting, the moan that escaped was only one of pleasure.

I reached down, and with a quick tug, ripped off her panties, leaving her bare against my knuckles as I undid my pants. A moment later, I was inside her, driving up into her as she cried my name over and over. This wasn't about

Domination or submission, about control or pain, or anything other than the fact that I simply couldn't stand being near her and not being inside her.

Only a few minutes later, I pressed my face against her neck, and buried myself deep, coming with a muffled groan. When she exploded around me a moment later, I wondered if maybe there was something to Erik's change of heart after all.

As I lowered Savannah to her feet, I pushed the errant thought to the back of my mind. I didn't want to go there. Savannah and I were enjoying each other, that was all.

I kept my face turned away as I picked up her discarded panties and shoved them into my pocket. As I straightened, I tucked myself back into my pants but didn't bother completely doing them up. I didn't plan on either of us wearing much of anything once we were done with dinner. Having her now had only whetted my appetite, and I knew it would take most of the night to satisfy it. If it could be satisfied at all.

"Would you like some champagne?" I asked as I gestured toward the kitchen.

She followed me, apparently lost in her own thoughts. Neither one of us said anything until we each had a full glass of champagne and were carrying plates over to the smaller kitchen table.

"I had an interesting call after work today."

I glanced at her, but she wasn't looking at me. In fact,

there was a strange expression on her face that I hadn't seen before. She took a drink from her glass, then raised her eyes to meet mine.

"Who was it?"

She swallowed hard. "It was your mother."

I stared at her, thinking I must have heard her wrong. She knew about my past and all the things my mother had and hadn't done. How she'd left me behind. How she'd chosen other people and herself over me. Hell, I even told Sav the whole truth about what happened with my sculpting. How it'd been my mother's birthday when I tried to surprise her with a present I made. How the guy had thrown it against the wall, nearly hitting me with it, and how my mom's reaction had been to throw it all away after the guy left.

Savannah knew all of that, and still, she talked to her.

"I don't know how she got my number, or how she knew I was doing a story on you, but she called me and–"

"What the hell were you thinking?" I snapped as I grabbed her arms, giving her a little shake. "Just because we've been fucking for a couple weeks doesn't mean you can introduce yourself to my fucking mother. What did you tell her about us?"

She yanked away, but not before I saw a flash of pain under the fury in her eyes. "Nothing. She didn't ask about anything like that." She took a step back. "All she wanted was to know if I could get a message to you, to ask you to call her."

Ever since Savannah and I made up after the incident at the restaurant, I'd ignored the handful of calls and texts I'd gotten from my mom. Every one of them said she wanted something. She hadn't even been subtle about it, though she hadn't said what this something was.

"I'm not interested." Everything inside me had gone cold at first, but I was hot again. "Why didn't you hang up as soon as she identified herself? Didn't you think it was even a little bit strange that she would track you down?" I held up a hand before Savannah could offer whatever flimsy excuse she'd planned. "Never mind. I already know the answer. You're a fucking reporter. Of course you can't mind your own fucking business."

Shock and hurt registered, and then it all disappeared. Her face went blank, and her voice was flat as she spoke, "Your mom said it was important. Life or death. I thought you should know."

"It's always important with my mother," I countered as I turned away from her. My head was spinning, stomach roiling.

How had things taken such a horrible turn so fast? I'd been planning a night of decadent pleasure for the two of us, and now I didn't want to even look at her. How could she betray me like that?

Or, the better question, how could I have let her get

close enough to me that it would hurt when she showed her true colors? How could I have believed that she was different from any other woman? Different from Bianca?

"Get out."

The words dropped into the silence, and I waited to hear her argument about why she wouldn't leave, why I should listen to whatever excuses she planned to give. Instead, I heard the click of her heels on tile, growing fainter and fainter until they disappeared. When the door closed, I knew it was over, and I only had myself to blame for all of it.

TWENTY-FOUR
SAVANNAH

Everett had spent the night at Cal's, so I'd spent the night drinking alone. Which was good, considering I hadn't been in any mood to listen to my best friend tell me that he'd been right. He tried to warn me. Lei and Lorde had too. They told me they wanted me to be happy, but I knew they'd never fully forgiven him for how he treated me before.

The moment he attacked me for speaking to his mother, I wished I'd listened to them.

I wished I'd never forgiven him, that I'd walked away when he apologized for his behavior. But no, I'd believed that he'd changed, believed that I could trust him. People made mistakes. Jumping to a conclusion once was understandable, even as far as Jace had taken things, but after spending nearly three weeks together, the fact that he could turn on a dime like that...

I took a slow breath and blew it out just as slowly. The cab's air conditioning was on high this afternoon – no surprise considering it was the first of August – and the cold air cooled me off as it filled my lungs. I'd gotten drunk enough last night to have a killer headache when I woke this morning, and enough alcohol lingered in my system that I was still a little nauseous. Worse, it meant that my emotions were still a bit too close to the surface.

I probably should have still been in bed, getting more hydrated and watching sappy rom coms with Everett, but the first thing I thought after the painkillers kicked in was that I had something I needed to do.

The café wasn't far from my apartment, but it was too hot to walk, especially when half-hungover from a fairly cheap bottle of wine. I ordered my usual Iced Chestnut Praline Latte, then looked around for the woman I'd come here to meet.

"Miss Birch?"

I turned to see a woman a couple inches taller than me, early fifties, but trying to look much younger. She was thin as well, but the kind that came from dieting too much to be healthy.

She didn't really look like Jace, but I had no doubt as to who she was.

"Ms. Randell." I put out my hand and she shook it. Or,

rather, she put her limp, cold hand in mine and let me do the shaking.

"I have a table over here," she said.

I followed her, telling myself that I'd done the right thing by coming here. Jace may have turned out to be an asshole, but I believed his mother when she said it was a matter of life and death. If anything, the way he treated me made me think that maybe he was overly harsh about his mom too. But even if he was correct in assuming that she was exaggerating the importance of what she wanted to talk to him about, I wasn't going to let him use me to blow her off.

I hadn't intended to stay, but something in her eyes made me think that I should hear her out. I hadn't been too happy with my gut's judgement recently, but I decided to trust it here. If nothing else, I'd enjoy my latte and have some closure.

When we reached the back booth, I was surprised to see that it wasn't empty. The girl had short, rust-colored curls, and the sort of pale skin that made me think she was ill. She also looked enough like Veronica Randell for me to suspect that Jace had a half-sister. One I was almost certain he knew nothing about.

"Miss Birch," Veronica began.

"Savannah, please." I felt too much like it was work when she used my surname, and despite what Jace thought, I wasn't going to use anything I learned here in my article. Nor did I have any intention of sharing private information with Ms. Randell.

Veronica nodded as she slid into the booth next to her daughter. "Savannah, this is my daughter, Iggy."

I wasn't a journalist as much as an art critic, but I'd spent enough time interviewing people for human interest stories that I'd learned to read how to best get the information I wanted from my sources. Veronica was practically vibrating with her need to share, so I kept quiet rather than asking questions.

"Jace doesn't know about her," Veronica blurted out.

Iggy flushed, her eyes flicking to my face and then back down to the table. Her eyes were hazel like her mother's, but there was a sweetness in them that I didn't see in Veronica.

"I'm not proud of all the decisions I've made in my life," Veronica continued after a deep breath. "But I love my kids."

I nodded even though I wanted to comment on how poorly she demonstrated that love with her son. It wasn't my place, and if I was going to be more honest with myself than I had been lately, it had never been my place. Jace and I hadn't been dating. We'd been fucking.

I pushed that thought, and the pain that went with it, to the back of my mind.

"I know I've asked Jace for a lot over the years, and it's mostly been selfish reasons, but it's been for Iggy too." She put her hand on her daughter's arm. "Her father's not a part of her life. I got involved with him when he was married, and when I got pregnant, he ended things. He gave me a chunk of money to stay away and never contact him again."

Judging by the lack of surprise on Iggy's face, this wasn't the first time she heard the story of how she'd been conceived, but the way her ears were turning red told me that it still bothered her. Veronica, not surprisingly, kept talking as if everything she was saying was merely backstory that needed to come out before she could get to her real reason for being here.

"A couple weeks ago, Iggy went into the hospital and–" Veronica's voice cracked, and it was Iggy's turn to comfort her mother.

"I have chronic lymphocytic leukemia." Iggy's voice was soft but unwavering. "It's...I need a bone marrow transplant."

"And Jace is your half-brother," I said, leaning back in my seat. Shit. This was not what I expected when I agreed to meet Veronica this morning.

Iggy nodded. "I don't know if he's a match, but Mom isn't, and my dad..." She lifted her chin, a familiar stubborn glint coming into her eyes. "I don't want Jace's money, and I understand if he doesn't want to meet me, but if he'd just agree to be tested..." She shrugged, looking as helpless as I felt.

"It's advanced." Veronica picked things back up. "So, the chances of her finding a non-relative match before–"

The tears came now, and no matter how shitty of a mother she'd been to Jace, I had no doubt this show of grief was real. Even if it wasn't, I wouldn't let a child suffer because her mother was immature, and her brother was a jackass. My own feelings and pride didn't matter, not when compared to this girl's life. I'd do whatever I needed to do to get her the help she needed.

TWENTY-FIVE
JACE

This sucked.

For the first time, I actually had true sympathy for what Alix had been going through this past month. He'd gotten involved with someone he shouldn't have and found inspiration in her...and then she left him, taking his inspiration with her.

Technically, Savannah hadn't *left* me, but she had betrayed me, so I counted it the same.

I'd already finished several pieces for the show, and even though I preferred not to, I'd use them if I must, but I was done making them. I wouldn't touch another piece of clay again. I shouldn't have gone back to it in the first place. I was a talented painter, and that would be enough. It had been enough for more than twenty years.

Except now I was back to where I was before *she* came.

Standing in front of my paint-spattered canvas, waiting for something to strike.

I'd been tempted to drink myself stupid last night, if only so I didn't have to think about what happened, but I'd been too cautious, too concerned that I'd lose sight of all the reasons why I'd been right to end things and I'd go after her. I'd tell her that I still wanted her, despite what she'd done.

So I hadn't gotten drunk. But I'd needed something to distract me. I considered going to Gilded Cage, but the very thought of being with another woman turned my stomach. And since art hadn't offered me a refuge, I turned to physical activity. I'd fallen asleep almost as soon as my head hit the pillow...only to wake two hours later from the most intense erotic dream I'd ever experienced.

That was pretty much how my night had gone until dawn when I'd finally given up on real sleep. Things hadn't gotten better once I got up though. I'd shoved everything related to sculpting into the studio closet and pulled out my painting supplies.

And that's pretty much where I'd been stuck.

When my phone rang, I was frustrated enough that I snatched it up without even looking at the screen. "What?"

There was a pause, then a familiar voice. "Damn, what's stuck up your ass?"

"Alix?"

"What's wrong?"

"Nothing." I closed my eyes. "Sorry. I didn't sleep well last night. What's up?"

Another pause, and I could almost hear him debating whether or not to push the matter. Fortunately, he decided *not* was the better path to take.

"Can you meet up in an hour at Café Carlyle? I have important news to share, but I want to do it in person."

It wasn't until after I agreed and ended the call that it hit me. Alix sounded *happy*. He hadn't sounded happy in a long time, which meant that something had changed. Maybe he'd started taking pictures again. Which meant that I had hope for my own work.

When I arrived at the café, my friends were already there. I'd had to clean up, and traffic had been a bitch, so it'd taken me longer to get there than it should have. Alix was beaming from ear to ear as I sat down, clearly eager to share his news.

"Sine's back."

All three of us stared at him, but it was the still simmering anger inside me that made me speak first. "How is that a good thing?"

His eyes grew darker, but he didn't snap at me. Instead, his voice got strangely soft. "Her mother collapsed. That's why Sine left. She didn't think to tell me until her plane landed in Ireland, and by then..."

His expression twisted with a dozen different emotions, not the least of which was self-loathing. Then he shook his head and took a long drink of whatever was in his cup.

"None of that matters, not anymore. She came back yesterday and told me everything. We worked it out."

"I'm glad for you," Erik said, tapping his thumb on the table. "Really, I am, but I'm not sure why this was–"

"She's pregnant."

He could have dropped a bomb and it wouldn't have had more of an effect. This time, it wasn't me who spoke first, but Erik. He only said Alix's name, but it seemed to jar his cousin out of the slight daze his announcement had left him in.

"She flew back as soon as she found out," he said and looked at each of us in turn. "And I proposed."

"Fuck," I breathed as the other two seemed to struggle to know what to say.

That girl had practically destroyed Alix by leaving him without a word, then she came back, announced she was pregnant, and now they were getting married. Was I the only one thinking this was an awful idea?

Erik leaned back in his seat. "I have to admit, Alix, I'm a bit surprised."

That was one way to put it.

"Sounds like you're rushing things," Reb added. "I mean, you've only known her what, two months, and she was gone for one of them?"

"Why do you even believe her?" All eyes turned toward

me, and any other time, I would've stopped there, but my head wasn't exactly on straight at the moment. "She could've been with some other guy, found out she was pregnant, and decided to try to pass the kid off as yours."

"Jace," Erik snapped.

Even Reb looked shocked, which was saying something because he was usually even more cynical of women than I was.

Alix, however, didn't looked pissed, which freaked me out almost as much as his little announcement had.

"I'm the one who fucked up," he said. "Rather than trust that she had a good reason to do what she did, I jumped to conclusions, lashed out, and made the stupidest decision of my life."

I almost winced as that hit way too close to home. "You at least asked for a paternity test, right? I mean, please tell me you're at least being smart about this."

To my surprise, he actually laughed. "You really don't get it, do you? There's being smart, and then there's having your head so far up your ass that you miss out on the best thing that ever happened to you." He leaned back in his chair, his expression growing even more serious even though the new light didn't leave his eyes. "I love her. I loved her pretty much from the moment I saw her. And I didn't stop, not even when I was furious at what I thought she did. It killed me when I realized what really happened. And when she forgave me, when she said she loved me..."

A lump formed in my throat as a desperate sort of hope twisted my heart.

"We're getting married in two weeks." He gave us a wry smile. "And then we're going to Ireland in the fall for a big Catholic wedding."

"Better you than me," Reb muttered, pressing the heel of his hand into his temple.

"You'll see," Alix said. "Just wait."

"Like hell I will." Reb reached for one of the appetizers. "I'm happy for you and Erik, finding these women you guys are head-over-heels for, but I'll be damned before I let some woman lead me around by the balls."

Erik shrugged. "Trust me, my balls quite like the attention Tanya gives them."

Reb rolled his eyes. "You two are pathetic."

"Perhaps." Erik got this disgustingly heart sick look on his face. "But she's worth it. Worth all of it."

Alix nodded in agreement. "When you find someone you can't stop thinking about, can't get enough of, when no distraction is enough, you'll understand that there's no excuse good enough, nothing that could ever come between you and the woman you love."

Nothing. Right.

But that didn't apply to me because they were talking about being in love.

I wasn't in love with Savannah.

I didn't fall in love. Not after watching my mother use men. Not after Bianca had used me and left me.

No, I didn't believe in the sort of love Erik and Alix claimed to have found. The fact that Savannah even spoke to my mother for two seconds had proven that she shouldn't be trusted.

Right?

I let my head drop onto the table with a hard thunk.

Fuck.

Fuck.

Fuck.

What had I done...again?

TWENTY-SIX
SAVANNAH

When I was sixteen, my four-year-old cousin, Patrick, died because no donor had been found in time to save him from kidney and liver failure. He'd been adopted as a baby after having been left at a firehouse in Indianapolis, so there'd been no biological family to get tested after he was diagnosed at just two years-old. My family had done everything they could, even loaning my uncle and his husband money to hire a PI to try to track down Patrick's birth mother. We'd all been tested to see if we matched since a single kidney and a partial liver could have saved his life, but none of us had. Because of Patrick, I registered as a living donor as soon as I turned eighteen.

I'd gone through almost all of the testing process two years ago for a ten-year-old with CLL, but her older brother made it home from his deployment before my donation had been necessary. He'd been a better match.

It was Patrick I'd been thinking of when I told Veronica and Iggy that I wanted to see if I was a bone marrow match for his sister. I promised myself that when it came back negative, I'd swallow my pride and call Jace to beg him to be tested. I didn't know Iggy, but I wasn't going to let her die without doing everything in my power to make sure she lived.

Except when my information was pulled up and matched against Iggy's, it was a match.

I started volunteering in hospitals after my cousin's death, and I'd kept it up when I moved to New York. I'd organized blood drives and marrow drives, done fundraisers and written informative pamphlets. Which meant that the moment I decided to do everything I could to help Iggy, I'd started making a list of all the people I met over the last few years. I might not have had the sort of money or influence that Jace wielded, but I had some personal connections that I had no problem using.

It was thanks to those connections that, what would normally have been a four to six-week process of testing had been reduced to Iggy checking in Saturday evening for prep while I checked in this morning for my own final testing and prep. The transplant would take place tomorrow morning, and I'd be home tomorrow night or Wednesday morning. I had no idea how things had gotten accomplished so quickly, but I wasn't going to look a gift horse in the mouth.

"You do know you're crazy, right?"

I gave Everett the best smile I could manage. Just because I was willing didn't mean I wasn't a bit nervous.

He grabbed my hand as he leaned onto the bed. His eyes were full of concern...and a little anger.

"That bastard doesn't deserve to have you doing this for him."

Okay, a lot of anger.

When I'd gotten home Saturday night, I told him everything, then made him promise to not go after Jace. The last thing I needed was for my friend to end up in the ER with a broken hand because he'd beaten the shit out of my former lover. It was only my request to have him at the hospital with me that kept him from being the overprotective big brother I'd never had.

"I'm not doing it for him," I reminded Everett. "I'd never be able to live with myself if a seventeen-year-old girl died because I was too pissed at the half-brother she didn't even know to do what was right."

Everett scowled, his fingers tightening around mine. "He didn't deserve you."

"I'll agree with you there," I said lightly. When he gave me a skeptical look, I continued, "We were both in the wrong the first time he blew up at me, but I know I didn't do anything wrong this time. Whatever issues he has, they're all on him."

A nurse came in and Everett excused himself to make a call. By the time he came back, she was finished, and he was smiling.

"You were talking to Cal," I guessed, happy for my friend.

"Guilty." He grinned as he plopped back down in his chair. "Back to–"

"No..." I held my two pointer fingers into a cross as if warding off the ghost of that topic. "I don't want to think about Jace or any of that. I'm doing the right thing here, I know that, and nothing is going to change my mind. What I need from you is a distraction."

He was quiet for a moment, then nodded. "I can do that."

"Good," I said. "Now, distract. Tell me how that amazing boyfriend of yours is doing."

The puppy dog expression reappeared. "He got that promotion I was telling you about last week."

"That's great!" I reached over and grabbed his hand.

"It is," he agreed, squeezing my fingers. "In fact, they gave him a huge account with the promotion, and he's going on a two-week trip to Greece in September to meet with the company heads face-to-face." After a moment's pause, he added, "And he wants me to go with him."

"That's wonderful," I said sincerely. "I'm so happy for you."

While I could see that he was still worried about me, the light in his eyes was one hundred percent genuine. The emotion that squeezed my heart was part joy at seeing my friend so happy...and part grief that I wasn't able to experience the same thing.

Maybe someday, but not right now. It'd be a while before my heart recovered enough to even think of being with another man. Anger hadn't burned away what I felt for him, no matter how much I might've wished it would have.

TWENTY-SEVEN
JACE

Why wasn't she answering her damn phone? Or at least responding to a fucking text?

The moment I left Café Carlyle on Saturday night, I'd been trying to reach her, to ask her to see me so I could properly apologize. But her calls had gone straight to voicemail, and the texts I'd sent left unanswered.

I deserved nothing less, I knew. The first time I acted like a jackass, she'd forgiven me. This time, I didn't deserve her forgiveness. She'd done nothing wrong. It had all been me.

It had occurred to me more than once as I waited for her reply that maybe I should walk away, should leave her alone. She deserved someone who would treat her better than I was capable of doing. Someone who wasn't going to assume the worst of her because of the other women he'd known.

But I didn't want to be that man anymore. I wanted to be a better man, one who might be able to eventually make peace with her. Be worthy of her.

My thoughts ran ragged through my mind, around and around, reminding me of all the ways I'd failed her...and of how miserable I would be if I couldn't at least convince her of how sorry I was. Even if I never won her back, maybe she wouldn't hate me.

I spent Sunday painting in the hopes it would distract me enough to keep me from calling or texting. Not artistic painting. I had no heart for that at the moment. No, I'd painted one of the guest bathrooms. It had been eggshell, and now it was alabaster.

On Monday morning, I went to Savannah's apartment, hoping to catch her on her way to work, but she didn't come out. No one did. I paced in front of the building, my agitation growing with every passing hour. By noon, when she still hadn't appeared, I reluctantly went back home.

Except home didn't offer the solace I wanted. All it had was reminders of what I'd lost. Rooms where I'd made love to her. Furniture full of memories of what it had felt like to be inside her, above her, behind her. And all those sculptures of her, of that amazing body, of how she made me feel. There wasn't a single one of them that hadn't been inspired by her.

Which meant I had no chance of escaping her.

And yet another night of broken sleep and dreams of her.

When I woke up, I knew there was one more place I could find her.

I WAS HALFWAY to Abel Updike's office when a stout middle-aged woman stepped in front of me.

"Mr. Updike isn't seeing anyone right now," she said firmly.

I looked down at her and reminded myself that nothing that happened was her fault. I'd gotten myself into enough trouble projecting my issues onto other people. I didn't need to take things out on this woman too.

"I need to talk to him." I wasn't rude, but I certainly wasn't backing down either. "Tell him I'm here."

Something on my face must have told her that I wasn't going to walk away, because after just a few seconds, she sighed and shook her head. "He's just eating his breakfast. I'm going to step out to get him some coffee. If you happened to slip inside while I'm out, well, there's nothing I could do to stop it."

I waited until she disappeared before I went into the office. Abel was behind his desk, the front of his shirt dusted with crumbs and sugar. He glared at me as I shut the door behind me, but didn't tell me to leave.

"Where's Savannah?"

He shrugged as he swallowed. "Not here."

I waited for him to elaborate, but when he didn't, I stepped closer to his desk. "Where is she?"

"Home would be my guess." Abel brushed off his shirt and pushed back from his desk. "But even if she was here, I'd tell you that she can't give you a preview of her article. That isn't how we do things around here. So if she promised you that you could have some sort of final say–"

I held up a hand and gave him a glare to back it up. "I just need to talk to her. You say she's at home?"

"I said that would be my guess," he corrected. "Or she better be, because I don't just let people take two weeks of sick leave if they're going to use that as a way around not using their vacation time–"

"Wait." My stomach dropped. "Savannah's sick? Sick enough to need two weeks off?"

Had I upset her that badly? That didn't sound like the tough woman I'd come to know. Something had to have happened since I last saw her. Something that had made her take that much time off. Had something happened to her family?

The questions hit me one after the other as I waited for Abel to give me some answers. When he didn't, I stepped around the desk. "What's wrong with her?"

"I don't know," Abel snapped. "Not my place to ask, is it? She just called yesterday morning, said she needed two weeks sick leave, it was important, and she'd have all the paperwork in by the end of the week."

I wanted to grab him and shake him. How could he not have asked her if she was okay? If she needed anything? Was he an idiot or just fucking irresponsible?

But I didn't do any of that, didn't yell any of my questions at him, because I knew they were directed more at me than they were at him. I should have been the one to know where she was and what was wrong. She should have called me to tell me what was going on. I should have been taking care of her.

But I was the asshole who'd been too caught up in my own shit that I wasn't able to see the best thing that ever happened to me had been right in front of my face.

"I need to talk to her – not about the article – but I can't get ahold of her."

Abel's eyes narrowed. "Mr. Randell, I don't know what you're playing at, but if Miss Birch isn't answering your calls, then maybe you should take a hint."

I ignored his sage advice and asked another question, "What about her friends? Where can I find them? Her roommate, Everett."

"I would assume you could find him at her home address." Abel walked around me to the door.

"And if he wasn't at home but rather at work..."

Abel scowled, but seemed to figure that the best way to get rid of me was to just give me the information I wanted. "He works in the NYU physics department."

"Thank you," I said as I left. I gave the receptionist a smile and nod, but my mind was already a million miles away, running through all of the possible things that could be wrong with Savannah, all the things I should have protected her from.

By the time I reached NYU and managed to find the right department, my nerves and my patience were both frayed. Fortunately, I spotted the familiar blond before I snapped at anyone.

"Everett!"

He raised his head, his pleasant face immediately twisting with fury as soon as he saw me. His hands curled into fists and wondered if I was about to get a black eye for my troubles. It'd be worth it though, if I found out if Savannah was okay.

"What the fuck do you want?" he snapped.

"Where's Savannah?" I blurted out the question. "She's not answering my calls or texts, and her boss said she took sick leave. I went to your apartment and she wasn't there."

Everett stepped right into my space. "Stay away from her."

I was taller than average, but he still had several inches on me. I didn't back down though. "Where is she?"

"She's in the fucking hospital, okay? No thanks to you."

TWENTY-EIGHT
SAVANNAH

I wasn't regretting my decision to donate to Iggy, but as my drug-assisted slumber began to fade, I was definitely ready to get out of the hospital.

My part of the procedure had been finished by early afternoon yesterday, but after a negative reaction to the anesthesia, the doctors wanted to keep me in overnight, which meant I hadn't been home in days. As I became more aware of myself, I realized that I felt better than when I woke up yesterday, but still, all I wanted was to go home and curl up in my own bed.

I'd had some weird form of post-operative hypothermia, one that hadn't just given me chills but a fever as well. I'd been groggy through everything, but Everett had been here, and I'd focused on his voice as he talked to the doctors. As he calmly discussed my reaction, I was glad I hadn't called my parents to tell them about the surgery. Mom would've been freaking out, and I probably would've been lectured about taking unnecessary risks. I loved her, but when it came to us kids, she always overreacted. Then again, I supposed having watched her brother go through losing a child didn't really make it overreacting.

"Her temperature's back where it should be."

A woman's voice I recognized as belonging to the doctor cut through the haze. My eyelids still felt too heavy to open, so I focused on listening.

"Once she wakes up, I'll have a better idea of when she can be discharged. I want to monitor her temperature for at least a couple hours when she's awake, and make sure she can hold down water and solid food."

Food.

I hadn't eaten anything yesterday, I remembered now. My teeth had been chattering and my stomach queasy, so they'd put some stuff in my IV to make sure I didn't get dehydrated.

Food sounded good. I wasn't so sure about hospital food, but I'd take anything I could get right now. When I got home, I'd have Everett get me all of my favorites. For once, I wouldn't argue with him taking care of me.

"And you really can't tell me why she had surgery?"

That wasn't Everett's voice, but I knew it. Why did I know it?

"You're lucky I gave you that much. Mr. Blount may

have said you were going to take care of things today, but Miss Birch is my patient, and until she says it's okay, I won't give you any additional private information. No matter who your father was."

That should have been a clue, but my brain was still trying to muddle through the last of the drugs I'd been given. So much so that it took me a minute to realize that if I opened my eyes, I'd be able to see who it was rather than trying to puzzle it out.

I heard the steady beeping of my heart increase as I gathered my strength and forced my eyes open. As the room slowly came into focus, so did the man standing near the doorway. Pale hair. Broad shoulders. Athletic build.

"Jace?"

My voice was raspy, his name little more than a whisper, but he turned as soon as I said it. His eyes widened, and then he crossed the distance between us in just a few long strides.

"Savannah." He went to his knees next to the bed, wrapping his hands around mine. "I'm so glad you're okay."

I stared at him, wondering for a moment if I was seeing things because he surely couldn't be here. Not after the horrible things he said. But I could feel the heat from his hands around mine. Could see the dark smudges under blood-shot eyes. So he was real.

"You look like shit." As soon as the words came out, I winced. Not because of what I said but because they made my throat hurt. Before I could ask for something to drink though, Jace was on his feet and getting me a glass of water.

I drank it slowly, hoping the cool liquid would help my mind clear. When I finished, Jace took the cup and put it back on the tray, then took a seat in the chair next to the bed. He leaned close but didn't take my hand again.

"Why are you here?" It came out harsher than I intended. I coughed to clear the emotion from overtaking my throat. "I mean, you and not Everett. And how did you know I was here?"

"Ah." Color rose in his cheeks. "I may have gone to your work and your boss told me you'd taken sick leave. I was worried, so I asked him where I could find Everett."

"Maybe my mind's still fuzzy from the drugs and everything," I worked to keep my voice even, "but that still doesn't explain *why* you're here."

"I came to apologize."

If I'd heard the slightest bit of arrogance in his voice, or even a hint that he was expecting an apology from me, I would've told him to get out, then had a few choice words for Everett for ratting me out.

But he not only sounded sincere, he sounded like he was...in pain.

"I don't even know where to start to tell you how sorry I am for what I said to you." His hands were curled into fists so tightly that his knuckles were white. "I won't make excuses, because I know that's all they'd be. Absolutely nothing is a good reason for how I behaved. It was childish, immature..."

He paused, and I raised an eyebrow.

"Go on."

One corner of his mouth twitched up, but the sincerity in his eyes stayed the same. "Juvenile, asinine, loathsome, despicable..." He put his hands on the edge of my bed. "I'll go through a whole thesaurus of words describing how horrible my behavior was, and I'll mean every word of it."

"Miss Birch."

The cheerful voice of the doctor interrupted, and the next few minutes were all about being poked and prodded and answering questions while Jace hung around in the hallway, pacing in front of the door. After I promised the doctor I'd eat whatever breakfast they brought me, she said she'd return in a bit to see if I was ready to be discharged.

While that should have been foremost in my mind, all I could think about was Jace coming back in and continuing our conversation. My head kept telling me to kick him out and call Everett, but if my best friend had already talked to Jace and *hadn't* kicked his ass, then maybe Jace had something worth saying.

"Is everything okay?" he asked as he came back to his seat.

I nodded. "Just the usual precautions."

He blew out a long breath. "I'd like to know why you're

here, what happened, but I'm not going to push. What I did was unforgivable, and I know I've lost your trust. I have to earn it back, if I can."

I wanted to tell him that what he did hadn't been unforgivable. He hadn't cheated, or hit me, or anything like that. He didn't want to give me excuses, but I knew that between his mother and his ex, his being guarded and assumptive wasn't entirely without cause. Still, it didn't mean I was going to jump back into whatever our relationship was with him without giving it some hard thought.

He reached out and put his hand on my cheek, his thumb brushing the corner of my mouth. "Even if you can never forgive me, I plan to do whatever is necessary to make things right between us."

"I want to believe you," I whispered as he dropped his hand.

"From the first moment I saw you, I wanted you." He raked all ten fingers through his hair. "But it was more than just physical, even then. We connected."

"We did."

"It wasn't until I lost you – until I chased you away – that I let myself admit what I'd never imagined was possible."

My heart began to race, and color flooded my cheeks as the heart monitor made sure Jace knew about it.

He didn't comment on increased pulse, didn't even look at it, but I had no doubt he could hear it. "Somewhere along the way, I fell in love with you. I don't know if it was when you laughed at the misunderstanding the first time we met. Or when I realize how amazing we were together, how well we complemented each other. Or maybe not until I began sculpting again and everything my hands made was you."

He fell in love with me?

He took my hand in his again and raised them, kissing my knuckles. "I love you, Savannah, and I will do whatever you want me to do to prove it to you."

Part of me wished this conversation could have come without us having gone through all the shit of the past few days, but another part of me wondered if Jace would have ever admitted any of these feelings if I hadn't walked away from him.

I could feel the tension radiating off of him as he waited for me to respond, but I didn't rush it. This was serious, and even though I was still in the hospital, I didn't want to postpone my answer. I'd rather take a little bit of extra time and be able to tell him the truth.

When it finally came, I knew it wasn't completely what he wanted to hear. "I love you too, but I don't trust you." His grip on my hand tightened. "I forgive you, and I want to work past all of this. It's just going to take some time."

He nodded. "I'll give you all the time you need." His eyes met mine, burning with the truth of everything he'd said. "Just don't give up on me."

Before I could reassure him, someone knocked at the door.

I looked up just as Veronica Randell walked into the room. She'd taken only a couple steps when her breath caught in her throat, eyes fixed on her son.

"Mom?" Jace stood so slowly I wasn't sure his legs would support his weight. He looked down at me, confusion in his gaze.

"You wanted to know why I'm here," I said quietly. "To do that, you need to meet your sister."

TWENTY-NINE
JACE

Two weeks ago, I'd been completely floored to hear one of my best friends announce that he was going to be a father...and a husband. I'd watched him pine for a woman he'd barely known and hadn't understood it until I'd broken my own heart by being just as pig-headed as he'd been. Now, it was the fact that I was standing in the courthouse watching Alix and Sine signing their marriage certificate that gave me hope.

That, and the fact that Savannah was here with me.

Everett had come back to the hospital when she was discharged, but I followed them back to the apartment. I'd checked in with her every day, talked to her, texted her. I'd brought dinner for her and Everett both when she said it was okay. I never pushed for her to spend time with me, but made sure she knew that I wanted to be with her whenever possible.

And I kept my hands to myself as much as I could.

It was hell to do, almost painful for me to be close to her and not touch her. I'd considered myself a master of self-control, but now that I was the one being forced to deny myself with no control over when the end would come...it was a lot harder than I ever imagined it could be.

Sometimes, I hadn't been able to stop myself from putting my hand on the small of her back as we walked, or tuck a stray curl behind her ear, but I always watched her closely, ready to immediately step back if I saw the least hesitation. Just like I'd done the few times I was unable to keep myself from tasting her lips. I felt like a man dying from thirst who'd been granted a few sips of water to help him cling to life.

I'd spent my whole life never needing anyone, always able to take or leave relationships with little personal impact. My friends had been the first to break through those walls, and they'd stuck with me after Bianca destroyed them, but I vowed to never let myself be that vulnerable with another person again.

But I'd never seen Savannah coming.

"Sine looks beautiful."

I looked down at the woman standing next to me and my stomach flipped. "So do you."

Alix and Sine hadn't wanted anything fancy, so we

were all in nice, but not flashy, clothes. Savannah, however, in her simple dove gray maxi dress, outshone everyone. It highlighted her gentle curves and made her legs look impossibly long for her height, both of which spoke to the artist in me as much as the man. My hands itched to run over her, to memorize this new image of her so I could translate it to clay.

"Not so bad yourself," she whispered as she smiled and held my arm a little tighter.

I didn't get the chance to reply because everyone else was clapping and moving to give the newlyweds hugs. Savannah and I followed and offered our congratulations.

"Good for you," Alix said in my ear as we hugged. "It's worth it."

I nodded. He was right. No matter how long it took for Savannah and me to work through this, being with her was worth it.

As she and I went to the limo Erik rented for the five of us, my phone buzzed. I glanced at it, a smile curving my lips as I read the text message.

Those are awesome! They're Savannah, right? Mom said not to ask you because it wasn't my business, but I told her that if you didn't want me to know, you'd tell me. Besides, I think it's awesome that she's your muse. Do you think you could make something for me when I get out of here? Nothing fancy or sexy like those ones of Savannah, but maybe something like an animal? A butterfly? It'll be a few weeks before I'm able to go home, so you don't have to answer now. Love, Ig

My mother and I were still working things out between us, but I loved Iggy from the moment I met her. The part of me that was hurt by knowing that my mom had stuck around to raise her daughter when she left me didn't touch my sister at all. All of that negative shit was between me and Veronica. Iggy and I weren't carrying all that baggage.

"Iggy?" Savannah asked, a knowing smile on her lips.

I nodded and pulled her closer to my side. "Thank you again. For stepping up and saving her when I was being an ass."

She stretched up and kissed my cheek before sliding into the back seat next to Tanya. While I hated myself for having treated Savannah badly, it was nothing compared to the guilt I would have felt if Savannah hadn't gone to meet my mom and subsequently saved Iggy.

I was going in next week to do all the paperwork to be on the donor list, and then I would plan a fundraiser where I wouldn't only be asking for money, but for blood. I'd given to numerous charities through the years, and had even donated blood a time or two in college, but I was going to put my money where my mouth was this time. Maybe I could do for someone else what Savannah had done for my sister.

This afternoon, though, I was going to celebrate with

my friends and use dancing as an excuse to hold the woman I loved.

I DIDN'T WANT to go home alone. My arms had been around Savannah more tonight than they had been since the day I fucked up, and instead of making it easier to let her go, it made it near impossible to even think about walking to her front door and then walking away.

"You know," she said as she leaned closer to me, "the doctors cleared me for whatever physical activity I want."

I swallowed hard, reminding myself that I shouldn't read into anything.

"And I know exactly what I want."

I closed my eyes. "Fuck," I muttered, my dick already growing hard.

She kissed my chin. "Yes, please."

I opened my eyes and kissed her forehead. "I'm not going to have sex with you."

She stared at me, disbelief in her eyes. She wasn't the only one who couldn't believe what I just said. My cock was threatening open rebellion. I'd gone longer than two weeks without sex before, but I knew that when it came to Savannah, nothing I'd experienced before counted.

"Why not?" She seemed more confused than hurt or

angry, more like the woman who'd responded to an accidental insult with a laugh.

"Because I love you, and you mean more to me than getting laid." I slid my hands down to the swell of her hips, fingers flexing at the thought of being inside her again.

"So, it's not because you're worried about hurting me?"

I gave her a half-smile. "Maybe that's a little bit of it." I lowered my head and brushed my lips across hers. "But it's more about trust, and you don't trust me. Not yet anyway. And I don't want to fuck that up by pushing you too fast."

She gave me a searching look, not saying anything as we finished out the song. Then something in her eyes shifted, like she'd made up her mind, and she took a step back. For one brief, terrifying moment, I thought I'd lost her for good, but then she reached out and took my hand.

Lacing her fingers between mine, she led me over to Sine and Alix, both of whom had arrived at their little reception looking distinctly rumpled and entirely smug. They'd also disappeared for about fifteen minutes less than an hour ago, and we all pretended like we didn't know what they'd been doing. At the moment, she was sitting on his lap, his arms around her waist, his hands resting on her stomach. The expressions on their face were matched ones of pure contentment.

"We're going to take off," Savannah said with a smile. She leaned over and kissed Sine on the cheek, then squeezed Alix's shoulder. "Have a great honeymoon, and we'll talk baby shower when you get back."

Alix's eyes dropped to our linked hands, then back up to meet mine. He grinned but only said, "Thanks for coming."

I opened my mouth to say something – exactly what, I didn't know – but Savannah beat me to it.

"Good night."

And then we were heading out the door. She gave the cab driver my address, then settled against my side, pulling my arm around her. A part of me wanted to ride it out, let her direct where we went and what we did, but another part knew that I wouldn't be able to keep from feeling like I'd taken advantage of her if we didn't talk.

"What are we doing, Sav?" I kissed the top of her head. "I mean, I love being here with you, and I'll stay as long as you want but–"

"I've decided to trust you." She leaned back so she could look at me after that rather startling statement. "So, don't do anything stupid again."

My heart gave a wild thud. "I'll do my best, but you have permission to kick my ass when I do."

"Deal." She grabbed the back of my neck, pulling me down until her lips were a breath from mine. "Now, I love you and I trust you, which means it's time for you to tie me up and fuck me."

I couldn't argue with that.

THIRTY
SAVANNAH

When Jace mentioned that he and his friends owned a place in Aspen, I didn't know why the first thing that came to mind was a cottage. I knew all four of them were loaded enough to buy homes worth a couple million, but aside from being mentioned once or twice in the six months since Jace and I had gone from *unsure* to *definitely together*, I hadn't really thought about it.

Then Jace had planned a romantic Valentine's Day week for the two of us, and I'd forgotten that the picture in my head most likely wouldn't match the real thing. I had a couple other things on my mind.

It was spectacular. Five bedrooms, so each of the guys had one of their own, with one leftover for guests, but it wasn't the number of rooms that made it so awe-inspiring.

Every exterior wall was glass, and with it being on the side of a mountain overlooking a river, the view was incredible.

"Do you ever get used to this place?" I asked as I came out of the bathroom, snug and warm in the plush bathrobe Jace bought for me.

We'd been here for three days, and I still wasn't used to it. Surrounded by the snow-covered Rockies and inundated with the scent of pine, we were wonderfully isolated, able to focus solely on each other. And able to do whatever we wanted pretty much wherever we wanted. Only the other guys' bedrooms and bathrooms were off limits. Which meant we'd had sex on pretty much every other available piece of furniture in the entire house.

"I haven't." Jace came over to me and wrapped his arms around my waist. "But it's become more beautiful with you here."

He looked over to where a pair of sculptures stood on either side of the fireplace. They were me, but more intimate parts than he'd wanted anyone else to see. I still couldn't look at them without blushing, so I was glad he decided to keep them.

His show had gone over spectacularly. Everyone had been shocked and thrilled in equal parts when he revealed his new medium. No one but me knew the true story behind the change. I kept it out of the article, just as we'd kept our relationship quiet until after the show. After that, we'd gone public and hadn't looked back. I'd written other articles for *The Heart of Art* and was now looking into branching out on my own. Jace was working on a new set of sculptures that were all about textures in nature.

Things were going great for both of us, and I hoped this was still only the beginning.

"When it's warmer, we'll go out there," he said as he led me over to the massive French doors that opened onto the balcony.

"We could go out there now," I said, leaning into his warmth. "Get all bundled up and walk out onto the snow."

He settled his hands on the belt of my robe, his breath hot on my ear as he spoke, "But I don't want you bundled up."

I shivered as he slowly slid the robe off my shoulders and tossed it onto a nearby chair. I could see our reflection in the glass, see the way my eyes had darkened. See the desire on his face as he looked at the reflection of my naked body.

"Put your hands on the glass."

I'd been fully aware of the glass walls before, but this was different. We were so close that if we'd been in the city, someone would have seen us. But we weren't in the city, and no one else was around. So, as he cupped my breasts, thumbs teasing my nipples, I let myself forget about everything but him.

A sharp jolt of pain went through me as Jace tightened his fingers, pinching my nipples hard enough to make my breath catch. His teeth scraped the shell of my ear, then nipped my earlobe before kissing his way down my neck.

"You are the most beautiful, most amazing woman I've ever met."

His lips and tongue whispered over my skin even as his fingers continued to roll and tug at my nipples, the gentle caresses and steady throb of pain at such odds that they merged into that intense pressure I'd grown to love, promising a huge explosion of pleasure.

One hand slid down my stomach to brush against the dark curls between my legs and I parted them, fighting to keep my eyes open against the rush of anticipation flooding through me. He'd introduced me to so many things in the time we'd been together, and I loved every one of them.

His two middle fingers slipped down on either side of my clit, the v putting just the right friction on either side of that bundle of nerves, even as his mouth and other hand continued their assault on skin still sensitive from the past few days.

"I'm going to get my cock wet in your pussy, and then you're going to come for me," he said. "And while you're still coming, I'm going to slide it into that tight ass of yours."

I almost shattered right then, his promise so sweet and so perfect. With the rare exception, I didn't want or need gentle, and tonight wasn't an exception. I wanted whatever he gave me, and I knew it would be what I needed as well.

"All right, sweetheart." The head of his cock pushed

against my entrance, and I shifted my hips, desperate to have him inside me.

I moaned as he entered me, my body stretching around him. I was so close, but I fought it back. One of Jace's favorite things to do was take me to the edge of orgasm and keep me there, forbidding me to come until he gave permission. The punishments when I failed were almost as delicious as the rewards, but I wasn't going to fail today. No, when he spent himself inside me and we were curled up in the nearby armchair, I'd tell him what I'd been waiting for the perfect moment to reveal.

"Come."

My body tightened as he drove deep and held himself there, the angle keeping him pressed against my g-spot as I climaxed. I called out his name, my hand slapping against the window as my breathing stuttered and my knees went weak.

Then the finger that had been rubbing my clit was pushing into my ass and my vision went white.

"Easy, baby."

Jace wrapped his arm around my waist, holding me steady even as he slid his cock out of my pussy and worked a second finger into my ass. The sounds I made weren't words, but Jace and I had been together long enough now that I knew he could read my body, if not my mind.

"Let's have a seat."

I barely registered his words before he was moving us

to the chair without missing a single thrust and twist of his fingers. Then he was sitting down and moving me so that my suddenly empty ass was positioned over his cock. My muscles were quivering, barely able to hold me, but he had me, just like always. As he lowered me onto his thick shaft, a strangled groan escaped. My hands shook as I grabbed onto his forearms, digging in my nails as the familiar but still overwhelming sensation of burning pain and pleasure raced across my nerves, invading every cell.

"Lean back."

My thighs came to rest on his as I took the last pulsing inch inside me, and I let him pull me back, changing the angle to something new. I fought to keep my eyes open, watching our dim reflection in the glass as he spread my legs. I flushed, but it was more arousal than embarrassment. My pussy was glistening and pink, my ass stretched wide around his cock. My nipples were hard and swollen, my throat and shoulder marked by Jace's teeth and mouth.

"So fucking hot," he murmured in my ear. He began to move slowly, a hand moving between my legs again to tease my clit as he made short thrusts into my ass. It wasn't hard or fast, but there was nothing *gentle* about it either.

"You're hot," I said, the words coming out as moans. "And I love you."

"I love you too." He caught my chin with his free hand and turned my head to take my mouth.

I could feel another orgasm coming, and when he slid

his tongue along mine, I moved my hips against his hand and then back to take him as deep into my ass as I could. He growled my name, then bit my bottom lip. The sharp pain tipped me over and I didn't wait for permission as I gave myself over to the pleasure.

I rode the wave as he played my body, taking me further and higher until he stiffened beneath me. He mumbled something against my skin as his cock throbbed and emptied inside me.

It wasn't until later, when I was in his arms, a blanket wrapped around us both, that I realized it was the perfect time to share my news. Before I could, however, Jace reached for something on the small chair side table.

"I meant it," he said, his voice hoarse and raw. "What I asked before, when I came."

I gave him a puzzled look. "I didn't hear you ask anything."

Relief shone in his eyes, and he let out a long breath. "And here I thought you were just telling me no."

"No?" I turned so I could look at him more easily, telling myself not to jump to any conclusions. "What, exactly, did you ask me, Jace?"

He held up a small box and flipped it open. My heart jumped into my throat when I saw the elegant twisted band and the flower made of small but exquisite diamonds.

"I asked if you would marry me."

Tears I hadn't known were lurking spilled down my cheeks, and I blurted out my own news. "I'm pregnant."

He dropped the box, then after a few long moments, took my face between his hands, expression earnest. "Say that again."

I took a deep breath. "I'm pregnant."

"Oh, baby." His lips were soft against mine, and then his hand was on my stomach, the touch different than anything I'd felt before. He rested his forehead against mine. "Is that a yes, by the way?"

I laughed and brushed my lips across his. "Yes, baby daddy. I'll marry you."

He laughed in return, his arms tightening around mine. "Good, because I prefer to be called *husband*." His cock twitched underneath me as he gave me a hard kiss. "Now, how should we celebrate?"

Thank you for reading *One Night Only* (*Jace's Book*).

Don't miss the other books in The Muse series:

The Billionaire's Muse (Erik's Book)

Bound (Alix's Book)

ALSO BY M. S. PARKER

The Billionaire's Mistress

Con Man Box Set

HERO Box Set

A Legal Affair Box Set

Indecent Encounter

Dom X Box Set

Unlawful Attraction Box Set

Chasing Perfection Box Set

Blindfold Box Set

Club Prive Box Set

The Pleasure Series Box Set

Exotic Desires Box Set

Pure Lust Box Set

Casual Encounter Box Set

Sinful Desires Box Set

Twisted Affair Box Set

Serving HIM Box Set

SEALionaire

Make Me Yours

ACKNOWLEDGMENTS

First, I would like to thank all of my readers. Without you, my books would not exist. I truly appreciate each and every one of you.

A big "thanks" goes out to all the Facebook fans, street team, beta readers, and advanced reviewers. You are a HUGE part of the success of all my series.

I have to thank my PA, Shannon Hunt. Without you my life would be a complete and utter mess. Also a big thank you goes out to my editor Lynette and my wonderful cover designer, Sinisa. You make my ideas and writing look so good.

ABOUT THE AUTHOR

M. S. Parker is a USA Today Bestselling author and the author of the Erotic Romance series, Club Privè and Chasing Perfection.

Living in Las Vegas, she enjoys sitting by the pool with her laptop writing on her next spicy romance.

Growing up all she wanted to be was a dancer, actor or author. So far only the latter has come true but M. S. Parker hasn't retired her dancing shoes just yet. She is still waiting for the call for her to appear on Dancing With The Stars.

When M. S. isn't writing, she can usually be found reading– oops, scratch that! She is always writing.

For more information:

www.msparker.com
msparkerbooks@gmail.com

CPSIA information can be obtained
at www.ICGtesting.com
Printed in the USA
LVHW081544080223
739012LV00002B/349

9 781981 454990